The Heirs of the
MEDALLION
BOOK TWO

CUTO

David Sage

The Heirs of the Medallion: CUTO
Copyright © 2014 by Mr. Sage's Stories

For information about this title or to order other books and/or
electronic media, contact the publisher:
Mr. Sage's Stories
www.mrsagesstories.com

ISBN: 978-0-9894210-2-7

Printed in the United States of America

Cover and Interior design by: 1106 Design

Table of Contents

With Thanks

To all those who worked so hard to expand the readership of *Adzul:* Deb, our greatest advocate in northern Wyoming, Beth for drawing in home-school and sports-team families in the Denver area, Jenny who opened her home one evening to the families of the entire fifth grade at Renbrook School, and the teachers who bought the book for every one of their students (you know who you are).

Special appreciation to Tara and Terri for supplying *Adzul* to the whole student body and staff of St. Timothy Middle School as a "One School, One Book" curriculum-wide project.

To adult readers in Story, and from around the country, who have enthusiastically "encouraged" me to finish the second book...here it is!

To my sons David, Tyler, and my wife Marcia, for your unflagging support as I transition from verbal to written narrative. Finally, to my daughter Tierney for your priceless counsel and editing contributions. I love you all.

David Sage
Story, Wyoming

Aztec Names

Coyotl	–	Coyote
Itzel	–	Rainbow Lady
Mazatl	–	Deer
Nenetl	–	Doll
Patli	–	Medicine
Sacnite	–	White Flower
Tenoch	–	Prickly Cactus
Xpil	–	Noble of the Fire
Yaotl	–	Warrior

A BEE BUZZED in the still afternoon air, lighting momentarily on the stalking warrior's ear, but the man gave no notice, brown eyes focused steadily on the figure 20 yards away sitting with his back to a tree. The murmur of voices carried from nearby gardens where villagers hoed their crops, but a screen of trees kept them from seeing the unfolding drama. With infinite care the brown skinned attacker took a step forward, toes feeling for any stick in the grass before he put weight on the foot. His jet-black hair was held in place by a red headband and he was naked to the waist, a long knife at his hip and a short spear in his left hand. A puff of wind stirred the leaves of the trees and, under cover of the sound, he took two quick steps forward then crouched unseen in the tall grass.

The man resting against the tree was also brown skinned but dressed in a simple white cotton shirt, with sleeves to his elbows, and matching knee-length pants. Leather sandals completed his wardrobe and he appeared unarmed except for a sheathed knife at his belt. His head was wrapped with a blue headband, but the shoulder length hair was gray and deep wrinkles at the corners of his closed eyes revealed the passing of many years since his youth. He shifted his shoulders slightly against the bark of the tree and the watching assailant froze.

Long minutes passed before the hidden man began to move, fearful that someone happening by from the village would discover him. Like a beast of prey he crept forward, hands moving the grass aside so there was no telltale rustle against his skin. Finally, he was 15 feet from the sleeping figure; two more steps and the victim would be his! He extended the spear as he soundlessly took a step, its razor sharp point now only 36 inches from the other's throat. One more step and it would be over. His pounding heart did not disrupt his intense concentration. He moved his right foot forward with the utmost care.

A soft voice interrupted the silence.

"Have I not told you, my grandson, that man is the most difficult of all animals to stalk?"

The warrior froze, foot in the air, before collapsing backward in the grass with a roar of laughter! "Not again, Grandfather! I can't believe it, I knew I had you this time!"

The old man opened his eyes, face wreathed in a smile.

"Since you were three years old, you've been trying to sneak up on me. When you were five, I let you succeed once, but only to encourage you! You've heard me say many times that a warrior must be tuned to danger every minute!"

"But Grandfather, we have no enemies here except the conquistadors and you have always said that they will be noisy and loud if they ever discover the village. You're the only one I can practice against because you have trained me so well that stalking anyone else in the village is too easy! Even my best friends, who trained with me, let their guard down!"

"Keep trying, Cuto. Your skills must be honed constantly for you never know when they will be needed! Now, let's see if we can find some rabbits or quail for supper."

With that, the spear was left against a tree and both men unwrapped long slings from their waists as they moved off into the nearby hills.

C H A P T E R   2

Solstice

GREAT GRANDFATHER chuckled, "Cuto tried to sneak up on Adzul for years but, other than the time when he was a young child, he could never surprise his grandfather, even as a grown man! The old Incan had trained as a warrior from birth and the instinct for danger never left him, even in his late 90s! Furthermore, although he had less strength than his grandson, he was still deadly accurate with the sling."

"It's amazing, he continued to hunt at 90!" exclaimed Juan. He paused. "But, then again, at 100 you're the most prosperous gardener in Center! I guess we shouldn't be surprised."

Seated around the beautiful kitchen table that Great Grandfather had made by hand, Juan and Sophia imagined he probably resembled Adzul as an old man. His face, the color of polished leather, was framed by white hair and there were deep wrinkles at the corners of his lively black eyes. He looked 30 years younger than his actual age and had the energy of a man half his years!

"Who were Cuto's parents?" asked Sophia. This morning was the first time they had heard the name and she wanted to understand the lineage correctly.

"Adzul and Itta had three children in the years after the village resettled in northern Mexico. There were two boys and a girl. The oldest boy was killed at 12 trying to defend his dog from a jaguar. The daughter grew up, married an Incan trader, and moved away. The youngest son was a farmer who stayed in the village, but he and his wife got sick and died shortly after their only child was born. Adzul and Itta raised Cuto who, like his grandfather, became more hunter than farmer. By the age of 10, he was proficient with both sling and atlatl, although the former was his favorite. There is no doubt that his grandfather and grandmother taught him to be independent; in fact, it was their influence that probably determined the history of our entire family!"

"The man we saw through the medallion this morning was young, it must have been Cuto," interjected Juan. "He looked to be around 20, just as you described him in the stalking incident."

"He left the same spring that happened," replied the old man, as his thoughts turned to the scene the twins had described not an hour before after braving the –15 wind chill to observe the sunrise over the Sangre de Cristo Mountains.

It was December 21, 1993 in Center, Colorado and, as the current heirs of an ancient silver medallion, Juan and Sophia were commited to look through its square hole at sunrise on the summer and winter Solstice. Six months earlier, they had been the first heirs in 500 years to whom the opening had revealed a scene from the past. Once again this morning, as they gazed through the medallion at the rising sun, the houses across the street were replaced by thick, blowing smoke. They held their breath.

Gradually the smoke cleared to reveal a desert landscape with low hills in the distance. Large saguaro cacti, some appearing to be more than 15 feet high, were everywhere and a profusion of colorful flowers covered the sandy ground. Six men and a woman appeared from the left, leading four donkeys loaded with packs. All were brown skinned and dressed alike with a sash at the waist supporting loose, white, short-sleeved shirts and pants. They wore leather sandals and each man's black, shoulder length hair was secured by a headband.

The slender woman was strikingly beautiful, with wide-set eyes above high cheekbones; her perfectly shaped lips revealed sparkling white teeth. Jet-black hair was collected in a single braid reaching almost to her waist. The man beside her was also slender but walked with the easy motion of one possessing great strength. His watchful eyes, and a slightly hooked nose above a strong chin, reminded them of an eagle on the lookout for prey. The two walked slightly in front of the others, evidently the leaders.

All at once the woman stopped and pointed. The twins clearly heard her say something as she ran forward. Jumping off a low bank, she splashed across a shallow river to the far shore. There on a patch of sand lay a small figure, face down, arms and legs flung wide. The woman kneeled and gently turned the body over. It was a young girl. She was wearing a dirty leather shift stained with blood and covered with dirt. Her right eye was swollen shut from a huge bruise covering the right side of her face. The bottoms of her bloody feet were shredded and torn.

But it was the ghastly wound on the left side of her head that caused the watching twins to suck in their breath with horror. A big flap of scalp hung over her left ear and, amidst the dirt and blood, they could clearly see the white bone of her skull. The woman cradled the girl's head in her right arm and raised stricken eyes to the men splashing across the river toward her. Suddenly the scene winked out and Christmas lights filled the hole again.

"Ohhh," sobbed Sophia, "that was so awful!"

Her brother lowered the piece of silver and stared at his sister with troubled eyes.

"Let's get inside. Great Grandfather will know what it's all about." He tried to sound reassuring, but his voice was shaky.

CHAPTER 3

Santa Fe

GREAT GRANDFATHER had listened intently to the twin's description before leaning back in his chair and taking a sip of coffee, eyes focused on the kitchen wall, a grim look on his face. He had fed them a hearty breakfast before they ventured into the cold and had steaming mugs of hot chocolate waiting when they returned. Shocked by what they had seen, the kids stared at him, the mugs untouched.

"At first I thought it might be Adzul and Itta," Sophia had ventured. "The young woman was clearly rushing to help the little girl and I remember Itta had a gift for healing."

"No," replied the old man somberly, "it was Cuto and his new wife Ria on the way north to Santa Fe; however, Ria also was skilled at healing." He smiled warmly to put them at ease. "Not to worry. Before we begin, though, I want to tell you a story about Cuto and Adzul."

There followed the ambush story. Calmed by his words, the kids had a good laugh over Great Grandfather's suspenseful description of the stalking incident. But the troubling scene they had witnessed soon came back.

"What happened to the girl? How did she get those horrible wounds?" Sophia couldn't shake the scene from her mind. "The woman, did you say her name was Rita, had a terrible look on her face as the others came up, like there was no hope."

Great Grandfather reached across the table and gave her hand a squeeze, saying gently, "You'll learn all about it but I have to start at the beginning. Her name was Ria, by the way, not Rita."

Juan wanted to pursue the details about where Cuto and Ria were headed. "Do you mean the same Santa Fe our family came from, north of Albuquerque?"

"The very same; however, it's only the most recent place our family is from. Our ancestry goes back to the Incan Empire in South America," corrected the old man.

"Of course!" Juan smiled sheepishly. "Qist was Incan and started Adzul on his pilgrimage north. But if Adzul was now 90, the time of this story must be around 1610. Was Santa Fe in existence then?"

"Very much so," laughed the elder. "The site of Santa Fe was occupied by the Pueblo Indians centuries earlier. The Spanish were latecomers!" The twins were silent for a moment.

"I had no idea it was that old!" Sophia was clearly surprised.

"Within the first 100 years after Columbus, Spanish ships were exploring both the eastern and western coastlines," replied Great Grandfather. "In the west, legends of 'the lost city of gold' drove them inland for great distances. Although travel was slow by our standards, they thought nothing of walking or riding for months in search of gold."

"Makes you wonder about all the problems they must have encountered," mused Juan.

"I don't think we can really grasp the issues of heat, cold, food, water, and sickness they faced." Great Grandfather was thoughtful. "Add to that navigating a totally unknown countryside, which often harbored hostile inhabitants! Throughout the early history of this country men were gone for months or years at a time exploring, trapping and trading. That any of them survived was often a miracle! For example, there are some estimates that up to 70 percent of the trappers died during the fur trading days in the early 1800s. Most trappers never reached 35 years of age."

He continued, "But, above all, the quest for gold has always driven men to extraordinary efforts."

"Like people in the 20th century searching for the legendary city of gold in the Amazon?" Sophia had been amazed at Great Grandfather's report of modern people disappearing in the jungle looking for the city.

"Yes. Even today people go into the Superstition Mountains of Arizona looking for the 'Lost Dutchman Mine,' reported to have a fabulous vein of gold."

"It's never been found, right?" guessed Juan.

"Correct," replied the old man with a grin. "That doesn't stop them though. Every once in a while someone claims to have found an old map that shows the mine's location and hope springs anew. Parts of the Superstition Mountains are incredibly rough and some folks can't let go of the idea that the mine is there somewhere, just waiting to be discovered!"

He went on, "Santa Fe was probably discovered by Spanish explorers seeking gold, but our immediate concern is how the family came to be established there." He paused as his eyes stared into space and his thoughts turned back 400 years.

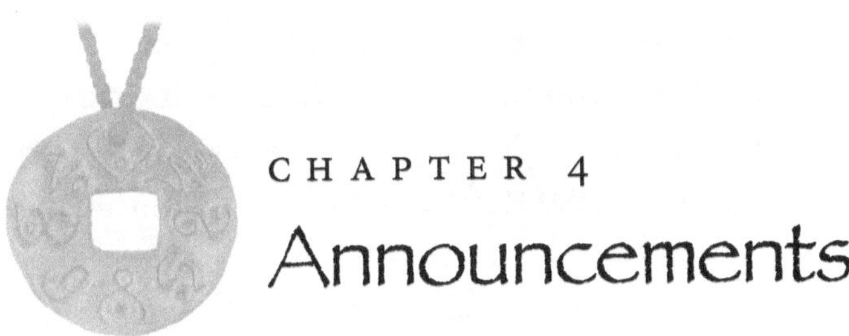

CHAPTER 4

Announcements

THE EVENING AFTER CUTO's latest unsuccessful attempt to sneak up on Adzul, they returned to the village with a deer slung over the young man's shoulders. Strips of roasted venison were added to vegetables from the garden and enfolded in tortillas by Itta's quick fingers, resulting in a delicious meal enjoyed by all three.

"We only need one quarter of the deer." Adzul nodded in the direction of the carcass hanging from a tree branch outside their small house. "In the morning take the rest and distribute it among the needy in the village. There should be more than enough to go around."

"Yes, Grandfather," replied Cuto, well versed in the old warrior's concern for the less fortunate members of the village. He had been taught since childhood that one has a responsibility to others who can't provide for themselves. The people in the community revered Adzul for his untiring commitment to providing meat to the elderly and sick. Although he was a capable farmer, the needy also benefitted from the love of hunting that took him constantly to the hills.

Now it was time for Cuto to make his first announcement. "I've asked Ria to marry me."

Itta clapped her hands, a wide smile lighting her face. "We've been wondering when this was going to happen!"

"You have?" Cuto was startled.

"Of course! The two of you have been like a pair of doves that can't bear to be out of each other's sight!"

"I didn't realize it's that obvious."

"Like the nose on your face." His grandfather chuckled.

Ria, at 19, was a year younger than Cuto. She was 5 foot 2 inches tall, 4 inches shorter than Cuto, with a slender and supple body. Long black hair framed a beautiful oval face with large brown eyes containing flecks of gold. When she smiled, which was often, perfect white teeth peeked from between gently curved lips. To Adzul, she was almost the exact image of the girl who had saved him from certain death by a jaguar years before and had later become his wife.

Cuto and Ria had played together as children but seemed to drift apart as adolescents. During the past two years, however, they had become inseparable. She often accompanied him on hunting trips and he would join her in the never-ending work of weeding her family's garden. No one in the village doubted that they would marry some day. When hunting with them, Adzul had noted with satisfaction that she had learned to use the sling and even seemed to prefer it to the atlatl or bow.

"We'll need to build you a house of your own," he said. "It's time you moved out from under our roof anyway."

That's when Cuto made his second announcement.

"We won't be staying here after the wedding." His voice was low. "We will be going north to the town the Spanish call Santa Fe."

"That's a long way, my grandson, what draws you there?"

"I can't explain it, but for more than a year I have had an increasing conviction that I need to go there. There's no particular reason, because my life is good here, but I can't get it out of my mind. The more I try to ignore it, the stronger it gets!" His eyes pleaded with them to understand because they were the only family he had and leaving them would be hard. "I also long for adventures like you had when you were my age."

"My adventures were not exactly by choice," the old man said dryly, but his look was kindly. "My father entrusted a great responsibility to the family and perhaps your move is tied to that duty. Your grandmother and I would never argue against such a powerful urge."

"Are the two of you going alone?" asked Itta.

"No. There are five others who want to go: Coyotl, Mazatl, Tenoch, Patli, and Xpil. We have been friends since childhood and if the situation is not to our liking we might all return."

Adzul stared at the young man. Cuto reminded him of himself 60 years earlier. He sensed there was little chance Cuto would return; if Santa Fe wasn't the answer, he would be drawn elsewhere. Instinctively he knew it all had to do with the medallion. His own journey had taken him from Pattiti to this hidden village in the hills. The medallion had been safe here, but now it was time to pass it on in accordance with his father's instructions. Its future was with Cuto.

"Because you have decided to leave, there is something I need to do."

He reached inside his shirt and pulled out the circular piece of silver with the strange markings cut into both sides and square hole in the middle. Slipping its leather cord from around his head, he extended the medallion to Cuto in cupped hands.

"As you know, my father gave this to me as he lay dying in battle. He told me that it possesses a great secret and that our family is to preserve it until the secret is discovered. It is a sacred trust that I am now passing to you. You must never be without it, and guard it with your life. In measure, it may protect you at times as it did me. Before you die, pass it on to the youngest member of the family with these same instructions. Do you understand?" The older man's eyes bored into those of his grandson.

"Yes, Grandfather." Cuto's voice was firm but he was startled inside. He knew that his dying ancestor had given the piece of silver to Adzul, but he knew nothing about its secret or the obligation to protect it. Before he could speak the old man went on.

"There were two other instructions. The first is that everyone in the immediate family of the medallion wearer be trained in the use of the sling until he or she is highly skilled. The second is that each person in the family be taught to weave the armor shirt. Until the secret is discovered, these skills are to be passed on to every generation. It was not by chance that I began to teach them to you at an early age. Ria excels with the sling but, now that you are marrying, you must teach her to weave the armor shirt."

"I will begin immediately."

"Good, your grandmother will help you; you will be well served if Ria gains the skill before you depart."

Cuto slipped the leather thong over his head and settled the medallion against his bare skin under the shirt.

"It's so light," he murmured, astonished that the silver piece didn't weigh more.

"One more thing," Adzul's words were measured and Cuto realized that the next revelation was extremely important. "My father's last words were for each heir of the medallion to look through its opening at the sun rising above the horizon on the morning of the summer solstice and again on the morning of the winter solstice. He died seconds later but I understood it to be a matter of the utmost gravity and I have been faithful to the instructions every year of my life."

"What have you seen?" asked the younger man.

"Nothing but the sun and the nearby surroundings," replied the old man, "but the medallion's properties convince me that, at the proper time, something will be revealed concerning its secret."

"In this, also, I will be faithful," Cuto pledged.

CHAPTER 5

Shirt

DURING THE NEXT two weeks Cuto and Itta spent many hours teaching Ria the precise weave required to make a shirt of armor. It looked much like the cotton shirts that the Aztecs customarily wore, except it fit more tightly and had a smoother surface.

"Your future husband knows the pattern perfectly well," laughed Itta, "but his fingers are thick and he is slow with the threads."

Indeed, the women's hands were quicker than Cuto's and the weaving of the shirt proceeded during the next 10 days. When it was finished, the three walked to a grove of cottonwood trees on the bank of the small river flowing past the village. Cuto attached the shirt to the trunk of a tree and told Ria to throw a spear at it with her atlatl.

"After all the work it took to make it? I don't want to damage my new shirt," she protested.

The other two just smiled.

"It will be all right," Itta assured her.

Still not understanding, but going along with them, the girl fitted a spear into the throwing stick and launched it at the tree from a distance of 20 yards. Her aim was perfect. The spear hurtled through the air and hit the shirt squarely in the middle…only to fall harmlessly to the ground! Rushing forward, she bent her head close to the cloth. A few threads were partially cut, but behind them a second layer of material was unharmed.

"That spear would have gone halfway through a deer!" She raised shocked eyes to the older woman.

"Incan warriors wore cloth armor that was equal to the heavy metal worn by the conquistadors," said Itta. "Its advantage is weight: in battle men can dodge and spin quickly and effortlessly while the Spaniards are slow and clumsy in their metal dress. Our armor can take a sword blow, or the thrust of a lance, almost as well as metal and it doesn't tire the wearer nearly as much."

"It's so thin," exclaimed the girl. "I can't believe it's so strong!"

"Not all Incan armor was like this." Itta nodded toward Cuto. "His great grandfather developed this particular type of cloth during the years he spent in the hidden city of Pattiti. It saved Adzul's life at least twice."

Ria glanced at the sleeveless garment. "If it had sleeves, we could use it in the wedding ceremony." Then she giggled, casting a look at her husband-to-be, "but I guess I don't need to be protected from you!" The words were said in jest, but the light in her eyes revealed her deep love for the handsome man beside her.

CHAPTER 6
Wedding

A WEEK LATER, Ria's mother, Nenetl, conducted the simple Aztec wedding ceremony. The couple sat side by side on a blanket, alone in the little one-room house vacated by Adzul and Itta. Normally, a house would have been built for them to begin married life, but their upcoming departure made that accommodation unnecessary. The older couple had offered their house so the newlyweds could be together until the time came to journey north.

Ria sat to Cuto's left and both kept their heads solemnly facing the doorway but their clasped hands nearly vibrated with happiness and excitement. Outside, the whole village was gathered and a few smiling faces of their friends were framed in the opening. Nenetl entered the room with a shirt over her left arm and a blouse over the right. Going to one knee on the colorful blanket, she gently laid the shirt in front of Cuto and the blouse in front of Ria. Moving slowly, to emphasize the seriousness of the occasion, she tied a sleeve of the shirt to a sleeve of the blouse, then rose and walked out. Cuto and Ria turned to look at each other and the love in their smiles elicited a murmur from the watching faces. When they stepped through the doorway a minute later, a huge shout erupted from the villagers and people crowded around to offer congratulations before attacking the mountain of food prepared for the celebration.

As they watched the festivities, munching on savory tortillas, Itta turned to Adzul. "Do you remember how my mother immediately liked you and wanted to care for your legs when we returned from the temple?"

He glanced at his legs, still covered with whitish scars from the terrible wounds inflicted by the jaguar's hind legs. "I think she was taken with my handsome face more than the wounds," he said, a twinkle in his eyes.

His wife snorted. "No, she wanted those gold plugs in your ears!"

When they had finished laughing, Itta continued. "I feel the same way about Ria that my mother did about you. I know that she and Cuto will be very happy together."

Adzul fingered the holes in his ears where the gold plugs had once resided. "That reminds me. I had better get our gifts for the new couple."

"Ahhh, yes," said Itta when he returned carrying two leather sacks. They found the newlyweds surrounded by well-wishers showering them with presents of clothing, cooking implements, blankets, and other articles needed to start their life together. After the last present had been given, and the others had turned back to the feast, the old couple approached.

"There were no instructions given by my father for these; however, I think it fitting that they accompany the medallion wearer." Adzul handed the smaller bag to his grandson.

Pulling open the thong that closed the neck of the sack, Cuto poured into his hand the two large plugs of solid gold that the old Incan had worn for many years in his ears.

"They're quite heavy! Didn't they hurt your ears?" He looked at the large holes still showing in Adzul's earlobes.

"I started with small ones as a child. Father increased the size as I grew and I never thought about it, although today I suspect they would be uncomfortable after many years of not wearing them."

"We will honor them as a family heirloom." Cuto replaced the plugs in the sack and handed it to his new wife.

"This my grandson, is a gift of a different nature. I've not needed it, but one never knows when the occasion might arise." With a steady gaze, the aged warrior handed over the second bag.

"It's beautiful." Ria stared at the soft leather. "What is the stitching on the outside?" She peered closely at the delicate blue threads. "It's the outline of a jaguar head! I've never seen anything like that, did you sew it?" She stared at Itta who nodded her head.

Opening the drawstring at the neck, Cuto reached into the sack and pulled out the skillfully cured head skin of a jaguar.

"Put it on," directed his grandfather, "it's a mask!"

The younger man found that the skin had been cleverly sewn together to create a mask that covered his head and extended to his chest. It was so ingeniously made that he could see perfectly out of the eyeholes! The lips had been stitched closed and the nose and mouth somehow filled out and stiffened to create the actual appearance of the cat. The ears were sewn flat on top of the head, in imitation of the way they would appear on a real jaguar about to charge. The resemblance to one of the big predators was uncanny and all conversation stopped as the villagers stared at the apparition that turned to face them.

"If I didn't know who was standing beside Ria, I would be terrified," exclaimed one woman in wonder. "It looks exactly like the body of a man with the head of a jaguar!"

"Itta made it from the skin of the second cat that tried to kill me. I've never had reason to use it." Adzul nodded toward a group of old men who had been in the battle with the conquistadors almost 60 years earlier. "I didn't feel it would help in the ambush at our original village because my intent was to give the appearance of momentary resistance and then flee. The mask might have caused them to hesitate."

"A bit of hesitation might have helped," observed his friend Yaotl. "The tip of that lance was inches from your leg when the first bola was thrown."

Choosing to ignore the jibe, the Incan turned to his grandson. "Keep it with you. It may be useful when you need an advantage."

Sports

"How's the elbow?" Closing the front door, Great Grandfather stared at the cloth sling holding Juan's left arm across his chest. It was the morning of New Year's Eve and the kids had come by for the next edition of the story. Hot chocolate and a heaping plate of oatmeal raisin cookies were waiting on the kitchen table.

"Still sore but coming along. Winning the tournament helps, especially when no one thought we had a chance!" After Christmas there had been a holiday basketball tournament in Alamosa. For three days, Juan's vastly underrated team had battled larger schools. No one expected them to get past the first round but, defying all odds, they had managed to advance by scoring the winning basket with one second left on the clock! The next two games had been against excellent teams from eastern Colorado but Center miraculously won both and found themselves in the final against Alamosa. Driving for a layup in the last six seconds, Juan had been tripped and fell into the net post, dislocating his elbow. The resulting foul shots, taken by another player, had won the game and the championship!

As usual, Great Grandfather had eagerly attended each contest but the injury to Juan had marred an otherwise perfect ending. Initially the coach thought the boy's arm was broken but X-rays revealed just a dislocation.

"When can you start using your arm again?"

"The doc says that I can begin practicing in late January and that I should be ready for the Regionals at the end of February. That should be interesting…"

"What do you mean?" asked the old man as they sat down in the kitchen.

"It seems some high school kids from Alamosa said I faked the fall to get the foul shots. They made threats about what they would do to us if we made the Regionals."

"I wouldn't worry about that, there are bad losers in every sport. All you can do is bring your best to every game and let the results fall where they may. Besides, February is a long way away and high schoolers have notoriously short memories!"

He turned to Sophia. "Think you'll get to play any after vacation?" Sophia was an outstanding volleyball player but the middle school didn't have a team so she played on a club team of older girls in nearby Monte Vista. She was also an alternate for the Center High School team.

"I'll play in Monte Vista, of course, because they need me to fill out the squad. The high school team is another story because there are two eighth grade girls ahead of me as alternates. I'll practice with the team but I'm not sure that I'll be asked to suit up for games."

Great Grandfather knew that the high school coach had already asked her parents about letting her play full time as an eighth grader the following year and simply replied, "Just work as hard as you can, the results will speak for themselves."

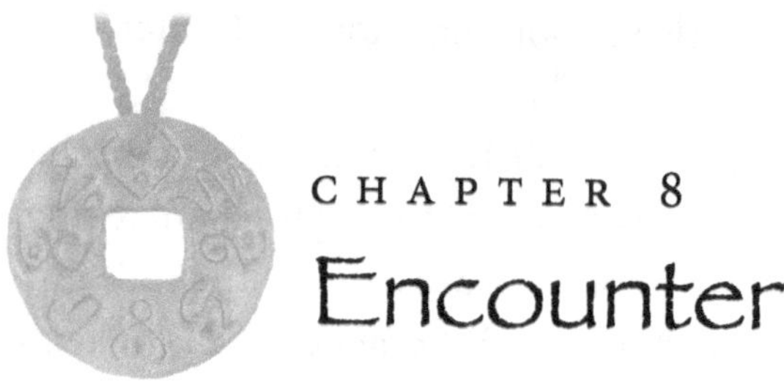

CHAPTER 8

Encounter

Cᴜᴛᴏ ᴀɴᴅ Rɪᴀ ʜᴀᴅ three wonderful weeks together before they set out with their friends. Four donkeys, piled high with supplies, trailed behind as they made their way out of the hills onto the high desert. It was late spring and the ground was awash with colorful flowers. Giant saguaro cacti extended bent arms to the sky and large birds coasted on air currents in the brilliant blue above. They camped at night on the grassy banks of streams flowing from nearby hills, beneath millions of brilliant stars. Freed of the set routine of home and farming, each traveler was filled with the exhilaration of setting out on a great adventure.

After several days, they came to a wide path running in a north-south direction. It was worn into the soil by extensive use, and along it, at regular intervals, were small piles of rock.

"This must be the trade route," observed Cuto. "It matches Adzul's description of the trail he and Itta followed north from the temple. Traders maintain these stone cairns over the years to show the way."

"Several months ago, a visiting trader told me the same thing," replied Tenoch. "He said sometimes the path gets washed out by flooding, or covered over by a sand storm, but the rock piles can always be seen in the distance to mark the course."

For the next three weeks they made good time on the traders' path. There was usually a stream at the end of each day's walk and there was always grass along its edge for the donkeys. By the end of a month they had traveled more than 400 miles north.

As the summer heat increased, they walked in early morning and late evening, resting during the middle of the day. It was just at dawn one day when Patli pointed out a thin plume of gray smoke rising straight into the sky almost a mile ahead.

"Perhaps it's traders," suggested Ria, grinning with anticipation at the thought of bartering.

Cuto nodded but didn't reply because he was distracted by a strange sensation. Under his shirt, the medallion was growing warm. Ten minutes later they approached the edge of a slope that dropped down into a small valley. The medallion was hot.

"Stop!"

Everyone halted and stared at him in surprise.

"Something is wrong, there may be danger." He spoke in a low voice to the men, "Get your spears and atlatls from the packs. Carry them like walking sticks as we proceed but be ready to use them. I'm not sure who is in the valley, however, I think we should be prepared." He turned to Ria. "Slip on your armor shirt and load your sling."

No one questioned the urgency in Cuto's voice and the weapons were quickly unloaded from the donkeys. Cuto and Ria concealed their armor shirts under cotton tops and dangled the loaded slings innocuously against their legs. If one didn't look closely, it appeared that the men were simply holding walking sticks. The donkeys were tied head to tail so that it took only one man to lead them and the party walked casually over the top of the hill and began the shallow descent into the valley. About 200 yards ahead, eight men lounged around a campfire beside a small stream. The trail passed no more than 15 feet to the left of the fire.

"Those are no traders," muttered Patli.

Even at a distance the little band could see that these bearded men were white skinned and armed with swords. A few had pieces of metal strapped to their chests and there were several long lances leaning against a large rock. As the Aztecs drew closer, they observed that all the men were extremely dirty, with ragged clothing, broken down boots, and filthy hair.

"They have no animals or supplies that I can see," murmured Tenoch. "I have heard of such men from the traders. They are soldiers that defect from the conquistador army and flee into the countryside, attacking and pillaging everyone they meet. We must be very careful."

When the Aztecs were 50 yards away, the unkempt men appeared to notice them for the first time. One soldier, taller than the rest and wearing a metal cap, stepped away from the fire and waved at them with a broad smile, calling out in a strange language, clearly inviting them to join the group at the fire.

C H A P T E R   9

Strategy

Cuto noticed that all of the soldiers were now standing, trying to appear casual, although each one had a hand on his sword. Several stepped in the direction of the stacked lances. He smiled and waved back at the tall one but began to give instructions to his cohorts in a low voice.

"We will go a little closer to get in range for our spears. When I stop, spread out to either side of Ria and me and pick your targets. Tenoch, let the donkeys go when we have taken our positions, we will need every spear. Do not throw at the upper body if there is metal covering it, Adzul always said to aim for the legs or lower torso. Give us room to use the slings; I will take the leader. Be ready to act when they attack!"

Although his men were farmers, every one of them had trained with the atlatl since childhood and was skilled at hitting a target as small and difficult as a fleeing rabbit. Unaccustomed to combat, their hearts were pounding, but Cuto's calm voice and instructions gave them purpose and focus. Each casually transferred the spears to his free hand, pointed down as though they were just sticks, and gripped the atlatl in his throwing hand. When they spread out in a line, targets were whispered back and forth without anyone turning his head.

Ria was terrified, although her face showed nothing. The conquistadors seemed so big and so menacing; she had seen the looks in their eyes as they stared at her before turning their heads away. How could they be stopped? Her sling hand was starting to visibly shake when Cuto's soft voice reached out to her.

"Remember the desert sheep, my love. You had to put a rock in the ear to drop them and you never missed. Choose the man to the right of the leader when they come and focus on his nose; an easy target because they all seem to have big noses!"

His humor broke the tension and she almost giggled out loud. Her hand steadied.

"Don't rush your throw, let the sling build full force, we are far enough away so there will be plenty of time. I am so proud to have you standing by my side and I will never let them hurt you. I love you."

The calm words filled her with joy and pride. Her whole body relaxed and her eyes suddenly blazed with intensity. These marauders weren't going to harm her new husband!

CHAPTER 10

Clash

The renegade leader had also been instructing his men in a soft voice. "These vermin have a lot of supplies on those donkeys. They are only armed with walking sticks. I will lure them to the fire and we will slaughter them, all except the woman, do not kill her! We will have a feast tonight!"

The soldiers, who had been without food for three days, muttered their agreement and studied the approaching Aztecs under lowered eyelids; this was going to be easy. The little group stopped 20 yards away, spreading out in a line facing them. One of the men, apparently the leader, raised his hand again and called out something in a strange language. Little did they know that it was both an invitation and a challenge: "We're ready whenever you are!"

The tall Spaniard smiled again and beckoned with his arm for the Aztecs to join them. Cuto smiled broadly but shook his head and repeated his statement. For a moment the two groups stood looking at each other.

"I'll cut off his head and feed it to the vultures," snarled the leader, drawing his sword, smile gone and rage contorting his face. "Get them!" he screamed in a hoarse voice, waving the weapon and sprinting forward. The rest of his men followed, shouting curses, blood lust in their eyes. A few snatched lances from the pile, thinking with pleasure of the bodies they would skewer like rats.

Xpil had the fastest hands and his spear was the first launched. The other four were milliseconds behind, aimed at different targets. The whirring of the two slings blended with the faint whistling the spears made as they hurtled through the air. Taking no time to observe results, Mazatl and Coyotl reloaded and sent missiles at point blank range into two men that had somehow survived the first volley.

The renegades were completely unprepared for the deadly barrage. In the blink of an eye four soldiers were down screaming, their bodies impaled by spears. The leader was sprawled dead 30 feet from where he had started, forehead crushed by Cuto's rock. Ria's sling had delivered a rock full into the face of the man running beside him, breaking nose, cheekbone, and jaw; he was sitting on the ground holding his shattered features with both hands when an Aztec machete finished the job.

In less than two minutes it was over. Seven of the eight deserters were down—dead or seriously wounded. The last man turned and ran for the hills. Sending Coyotl and Tenoch after the fleeing soldier, Cuto and the others put the wounded out of their misery.

"It's more merciful than letting them bleed to death in the sun or, worse, having the vultures, coyotes, and ants get them," he explained to Ria.

When it was over, the Aztecs made their way upstream 100 yards and collapsed on the grass, completely drained. Cuto lay with arms tight around his wife, her head on his chest. Cool as a cucumber when the fight started, she was sobbing uncontrollably with release from the tension. He stroked her head over and over, whispering of his pride and love for her, until her body started to relax and the sobbing gradually ceased. Xpil, Patli, and Mazatl sat with arms on knees, staring at the rippling water with unseeing eyes. Finally, spent with emotion, they all dozed in the morning sun until their companions returned.

The fleeing renegade was surprisingly fast and covered two miles before they trapped him in a small draw.

"He was no coward and charged when he realized he couldn't escape," reported Coyotl.

Two spears from the deadly atlatls quickly ended his attack and the body was left to wild animals.

Adapting

"Whew! Those guys didn't mess around, did they?" Juan shook his head in amazement. "As farmers they weren't used to that sort of thing!" Two weeks had gone by before they had a free Saturday for their relative to continue the story.

"Life was dangerous in those days." Great Grandfather looked at the twins over his mug of coffee. "It's hard to imagine in modern times, but one had to be prepared for anything, whether you were a farmer or not. Of course, there were many days and weeks when nothing out of the ordinary happened, but the ancient people were always vigilant. It's sort of like the way we look each way before we step into the street. The only difference is that the oncoming driver in our time generally has no deliberate intention to hit us. Back then, strangers weren't always so well intentioned!"

"It must have been a difficult way to live." Sophia ventured.

"Perhaps, from our perspective," replied the old man. "But it was second nature to them. Just as it is second nature for us to see planes in the sky, hear trucks roar down the highway, or note a siren going off. Those things would have terrified them! It's all about the times people live in; humans have an incredible ability to adapt."

"Modern animals have to adapt too," said Juan. "I read about a wolf pack that lives just a few miles from the city of Milan, Italy, right in the middle of farming country, but practically no one knows it's there!"

"I'm not surprised. Did you know that there are leopards roaming inside Nairobi, Kenya? It's a city like Denver in which leopards hunt domestic dogs at night. They are rarely, if ever, seen during the day!"

Sophia stared at her relative. "You can't be serious, in the city itself? That's dangerous!"

Her thoughts turned back to the story. "When you think about it, the medallion was crucial in warning Adzul of danger and now you're describing the same thing for Cuto."

Great Grandfather nodded. "That's correct. If it weren't for the medallion, some of our ancestors might have died at an early age; we might not have been sitting here! You could say by protecting the family it's been preserving its secret."

"Do you really think we will be the ones to discover the secret?" asked Sophia.

"For 500 years, each person wearing the medallion has looked through it at the rising sun on the summer and winter solstices but no one has seen anything until you two came along...and you've seen into the past twice! It must mean something."

"Sophia has no volleyball practice next Saturday morning and I'm still in rehab; can you go on with the story?" Juan was anxious to see what would happen next.

"Come for breakfast at 8:00 and we'll continue." His eyes twinkled as they headed out the door. He well remembered his own fascination with the family history when he heard it the first time.

C H A P T E R 1 2

Deformity

IT WAS MID-MORNING when the Aztecs, having recovered sufficiently from the stress of combat, returned to the conquistadors' campsite. They gathered up all the swords and lances, snapping the blades off on rocks in anticipation of using them for knives and spearheads. The rest of the metal objects were buried deep in the ground some distance away. The corpses were so infested with lice and fleas that Cuto decided to burn them to avoid infection for anyone passing by. Collecting wood and brush from beside the stream, they built a huge funeral pyre, adding to it every scrap of flammable equipment.

While they worked, Cuto and the men discussed how lucky they were that the renegade conquistadors didn't have horses. Adzul had told his grandson stories passed on from Itta's father of a few mounted Spaniards defeating great numbers of Aztec foot soldiers at Tenochtitlan.

"If these men had had horses, we would all be dead by now," Coyotl observed grimly.

As the bodies were piled up, Mazatl noticed one with a strange deformity: the left foot angled almost 45 degrees to the side from normal.

"How could he keep up with the others?" questioned Tenoch. "He must have had a terrible limp."

They all wondered whether it was a natural condition, or caused by a recent wound, but no one cared to take the boot off to investigate!

The entire area was swept clean with brush and everyone scrubbed their hands and arms vigorously with sand and water to rid themselves of all contact with the dead. When the donkeys had been collected and the group was ready to move, Cuto set fire to the enormous brush pile. In minutes, flames were leaping 15 feet in the air and black smoke billowed into the blue sky.

"No one will know what happened here, although they may wonder about the charcoal and bones," remarked Xpil somberly as they set their faces toward the north.

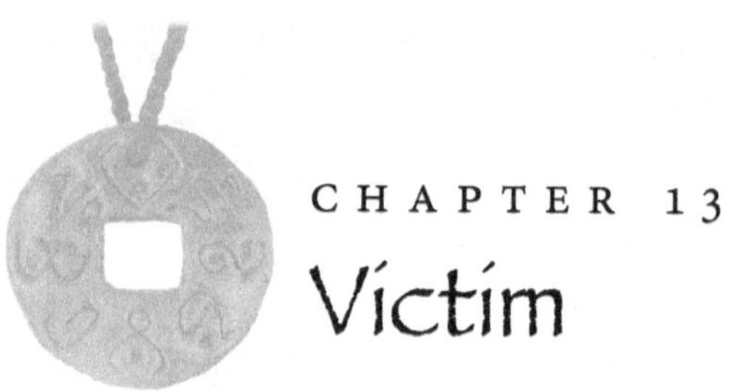

CHAPTER 13

Victim

THREE DAYS LATER, as the Aztecs approached a small river, Ria's sharp eyes spotted a figure sprawled on the far bank.

"I think that's a child," she cried, running ahead and splashing through the water to kneel at the side of the body.

Upon gently rolling it over, she discovered an Indian girl about 10 years old. At first she thought the child was dead because the body was completely limp, jaw slack, and there was no eye movement. Moreover, a vicious gash above her left ear, exposing the skull bone, could well have been fatal. Dried blood completely covered the child's face and the front of her short leather dress; a severe beating had left massive bruises on her face, swelling the right eye completely shut. Her bare feet were torn and covered with blood; clearly she had run a long way over the rocky desert ground.

"I'm afraid she's dead," Ria exclaimed as Cuto splashed through the river to join her.

"Who would do this to a child?" His eyes glittered with shock and anger as he took in the wounds.

The woman bent low over the open mouth and put her hand on the girl's neck. The softest breath of air caressed her check and under her fingers was an erratic pulse!

"She's alive! Bring a damp cloth and a gourd."

With the cloth Ria gently began to clear the blood from the girl's face. Tears welled in her eyes as she saw that it was thin and pinched with starvation. She turned her attention to the head wound and, with the greatest care, washed off the dirt covering it. As she worked she asked the men to build a fire and heat some water. When she was done, she carried the unconscious girl across the river to the camp they had made and laid her on a blanket. The others gathered around, drawn by compassion to the injured child.

"Search the supplies and find me the thinnest needle we have and a length of sinew." She pointed to a large piece of scalp flopped over the left ear. "I'll have to sew this scalp back in place."

Patli returned in a few minutes with the requested items, plus a razor sharp piece of sword blade taken from the battle. He helped Cuto and Tenoch hold the girl's head and body while Ria first shaved off the hair at the edges of the wound and then stitched the scalp together and bandaged the wound with clean strips of cloth wrapped around her head. She then bathed and bandaged the lacerated feet with poultices of honey and herbs.

Cutting away the filthy leather shift, Ria began to wash grime and dirt off the body with warm water.

"This girl's been whipped," she cried.

Against her newly cleaned skin, numerous white scars were visible on her back and legs. The watching men were silent, but clenched jaws and pursed lips revealed the emotions they felt about the brutal treatment the little girl had received. Ria gently eased one of her own shirts over the child's head and carried her to the shade of a nearby cottonwood grove, marveling at how light she was.

"Try some water," said Cuto, bringing a full gourd. "She looked like she was trying to crawl to the river."

His wife carefully lifted the girl's head and poured a trickle into her mouth. Most of it ran down her chin, but suddenly there was a reflexive movement in the throat and the child swallowed, her good eye popping open with fear. Ria crooned softly and smiled down at her. It took a moment for the child to comprehend that the woman's face was friendly before her fright subsided and she took two more swallows of water. In another minute she had passed out again.

"You may have saved her life." Cuto knew that Ria was familiar with treating wounds and sickness, but her quick action and skill had caught him by surprise. He was very proud of her.

"I think we should camp here for a few days to see if she recovers." Ria was still not certain that the Indian would survive the head wound. Whoever had caused it clearly thought the girl would die; otherwise she would have been finished off with a spear or knife.

"I've already told the others that we will be here for a while. It's a good spot because there's shade, grass for the donkeys, and plenty of wood. Game should be plentiful along the river and Xpil took Patli to see what they could find."

His assessment proved accurate as the hunters returned shortly with a fat desert sheep taken while drinking. Steaks were soon roasting over the fire while other meat was cut into strips to dry for jerky in the days ahead. Everyone welcomed the rest; they were all still feeling the stress of the fight with the renegades. That night Cuto and Ria slept on either side of the girl, prepared to respond to the slightest sign of consciousness but she never stirred.

CHAPTER 14
Healing

In the morning Ria made soup from small bits of meat, dried corn, and herbs. Gently propping her up with an arm under the shoulders, she trickled a little soup into the girl's mouth. There was an immediate reaction: her good eye flew open in fear, but she relaxed as she saw the friendly smile. Both hands reached for the gourd and she took several gulps of the warm liquid before Ria tenderly stopped her.

"Not too much little one, your stomach is probably so shrunken that it can't take more. I'll get you some water."

It was clear that the girl didn't understand, but her eyes never strayed from Ria's figure as she went to get water. After two or three swallows, she laid her head back on the blanket, one hand gently exploring the bandage over her ear. Shortly she was fast asleep again, but her breathing was steady and deep.

"I think she'll make it," commented Cuto from beside the tree where he had hidden so as not to scare the patient. "The rest of us will stay at a distance until she knows we mean her no harm. Those injuries could have come from a woman but I think not. A woman wouldn't have left her alive. It was a man and he just assumed she was dead."

At mid-afternoon the girl woke again and ate every bit of food Ria allowed her, clearly wanting more. But the Aztec knew what she was doing. Too much food would simply cause vomiting and slow the recovery. After eating, the child stayed awake for a while and began to take notice of the camp. The wary look in her eyes as she observed the men bore out Cuto's speculation about her assailant, and all six made a practice of deliberately smiling at her as they went about their business. In the evening Ria permitted a bit more food; she hated to take the bowl away because it was clear the child had almost starved to death.

Recovery progressed rapidly with Ria monitoring the increase in food until she was sure the girl's system could handle what her enormous appetite desired! Four days after they found her, she was hobbling on bandaged feet around the camp after Ria, the older woman's shirt covering her small frame like a dress. It was obvious the men made her nervous so they appeared to take no notice while, in reality, studying her closely. They were curious about such a brutal attack on one so young and how she had survived. She had obviously come a long way after being left for dead; they had backtracked her meandering trail for hours until the footprints disappeared on the rock surface of a large mesa.

The mystery started to unravel when Ria began talking to the girl through signs, the universal language among ancient peoples. Soon they were sitting together under the trees, hands flying, occasionally erupting into soft laughter together. At night, Ria filled the others in as the child slept.

"Her name is Swallow and she is a member of the Pueblo people. Two years ago she was captured by marauding Comanche and made a slave. Her life with them was hard. There were many beatings and abuses because she was not submissive and frequently tried to escape. Her owner, an old woman, tied her to a stake every night and made her sleep on the ground outside with no blanket regardless of the weather; she was given little food and often whipped without cause. Recently, she stole a piece of sharp bone from the embers of a cooking fire and concealed it under her dress. About 10 days ago the owner received some meat from her son, a warrior of the camp, and that night Swallow used the bone to cut the leather strap tying her, stole the meat, and fled into the desert.

"She ate all of the meat in the first two days, giving her strength to run, but the desert rocks began to take a toll on her feet and by the third day she was reduced to a slow trot. At the end of the fourth day the son caught up to her. She expected a severe beating before being returned to the old woman but it was not to be.

"'My mother never liked you and doesn't want you back,' he said in a cold voice, punching her in the face as hard as he could. 'She told me to kill you.' With that, he picked up a large rock and slammed it into the side of her head.

"He left her for dead but she awoke hours later. Determined to get home, she began to search for water, unable to see out of the right eye and half delirious from the head wound. She has no idea how much time passed; she would regain consciousness where she had collapsed and struggle on until she collapsed again. She actually smelled the dampness of the river before she saw it, but by then she was reduced to crawling and never actually made it to the water."

The men were silent for a moment, staring at the little figure, wrapped in a blanket, sleeping peacefully.

"She is very strong," said Cuto, awe in his voice. "Not many would have survived such an ordeal."

CHAPTER 15

Courage

GREAT GRANDFATHER pushed back from the table, indicating the story was over for that day. For a moment there was dead silence as the twins thought about what he had told them. Then Sophia let out a long sigh.

"What we saw through the medallion gave no clue about her terrific struggle for survival. Three years ago I was exactly her age and I can't imagine myself doing what she did. I would have given up and died where I was caught."

Juan could only nod in agreement.

Great Grandfather stared at them reflectively. "I think you underestimate yourselves. People often rise to the occasion when faced with extreme circumstances."

"Our life is easy. We never have to face life and death situations!" Sophia countered.

"You did pretty well with the cougar last fall."

"Yes, but we had the slings."

"What would have happened if you had panicked and run?"

"It would have gotten one of us," Juan admitted. "That would have been bad."

The old man was silent for a minute. "Have you ever heard of Sir Ernest Shackleton?"

"No." Their faces were blank.

"He was an Arctic explorer from England at the beginning of the 20th century. On an expedition to the Antarctic, his ship became trapped by ice in the Weddell Sea off the northwest coast in January of 1915. He and the 28-man crew spent almost a year on board before the ice finally crushed the hull and they had to abandon ship. They saved three small boats and all their supplies before the vessel disappeared under the ice. They survived on the ice pack for six months before they were able to get off and sail in the dangerously overloaded little boats to Elephant Island. It is an uninhabited piece of rock, with only two small, unconnected beaches; somehow, in a frightful storm, they all made it to the same beach.

"Knowing that they would never be found, Shackleton set out 10 days later for a whaling station on South Georgia Island, almost 800 miles away. He took five men, all experienced sailors, in a 20-foot boat with two tiny sails. They had only a primitive sextant to take a reading on the sun to give them their location. No GPS, no short wave radio, no satellite phone—those things had not even been imagined in 1916. The problem was that they hardly saw the sun because of the storms; the Weddell Sea is arguably the roughest ocean in the world. In his autobiography Shackleton describes a wave, which came at them from behind one night, so big that he thought the foam at the top was clouds reflecting moonlight! After two weeks, and mostly by dead reckoning, they reached South Georgia Island. This would be like you finding a lost contact lens in a football field!

"That's not all. They had to land on the wrong side of the island because a severe hurricane prevented them from sailing around it. Three of the men were in bad shape so, after a short time of rest, Shackleton set out with the other two, 50 feet of rope and a carpenter's chisel. In 36 hours they crossed 32 miles of snow covered mountains to reach the whaling station. The men at the station said they were almost unrecognizable as human beings! The three companions were rescued immediately, but it took four trips before they could break through the storms to Elephant Island; by then the men had been there 4½ months. The amazing part of the story is, during nearly 20 months of unbelievable hardship, not one crewmember was lost!"

The twins just stared at him.

"How do you know about these things Great Grandfather?" Sophia was amazed.

"I read a lot. The library can get almost anything I want and the Internet is an amazing source of material."

"We never hear about this sort of survival in school!"

"Read more and you will! It's all there in print, either electronic or paper." He gestured toward the living room where one whole wall was covered by a bookcase filled with volumes. "Truth is better than fiction any day! Real people have experienced situations that Hollywood could never conceive! I love reading about what men and women have overcome in the past!"

"It's just that we're not conditioned for anything like what Swallow or Shackleton went through," Juan remarked glumly.

The old man smiled reassuringly. "Human courage and willpower are absolutely amazing. I have no doubt the two of you will surprise yourselves if you ever encounter a crisis."

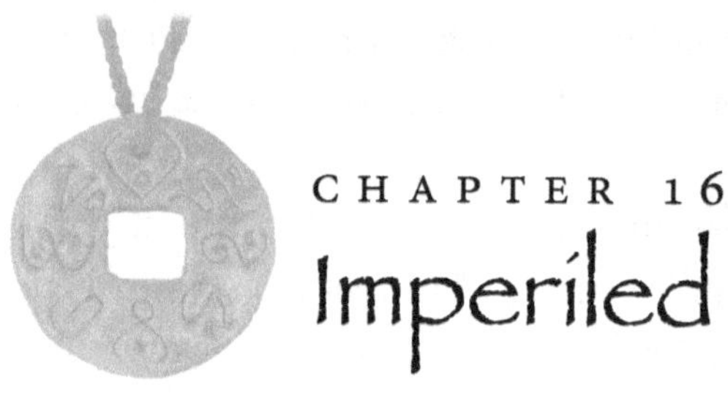

CHAPTER 16

Imperiled

BY THE END OF A WEEK Swallow was well enough to travel and they set out again, traveling slowly to accommodate her injuries. The trail now followed the river and several days later they camped in a grove of trees at the water's edge. Cuto and Patli set out to hunt the nearby hills and returned at dark with the body of a wild pig; strips of pork were soon roasting over the fire.

"This animal is quite a bit larger than a javelina," commented Coyotl. "I've heard that pigs often escape from the conquistador settlements and turn wild, perhaps it means we are getting close to the village."

"You might be right," remarked Cuto. "Tomorrow we'll begin scouting ahead as an extra precaution."

The rising moon was so bright they could clearly see the surrounding landscape as they settled down for the night. Sparks drifted skyward from the dying fire to disappear among the millions of stars shining in the cold desert air. Swallow lay close to Cuto and Ria, still apprehensive about the Comanche in spite of Ria's attempts to reassure her that the old woman had been glad to get rid of her stubborn slave and thought her dead. Soon the only sound was soft breathing from the figures wrapped in warm blankets scattered about the ground.

The faintest hint of gold was just beginning to show on the eastern horizon when Cuto abruptly woke. The medallion was warm! Without stirring, he peered into the darkness surrounding the camp. Nothing moved. A coyote yipped from the nearby hills and another answered from just upstream. When an owl softly hooted behind him, he knew that it was time to move. Intimately familiar with wild animals, he knew that these sounds came too close together to be natural; there were humans just outside the trees.

Touching Ria's shoulder, he breathed in her ear, "Get up slowly and load your sling, there are people around the camp."

She was instantly awake and quickly grabbed the sling while slowly rising to her feet. All she could think about was Swallow's fear that the Comanche would somehow come for her. Heads rose from the forms lying around the dead campfire as Cuto whispered a warning. Soon all were standing, weapons in hand, only Swallow slept on undisturbed.

The growing light revealed nothing unusual, but the normal chirping of waking birds was missing and the still air was filled with almost palpable tension. The seven Aztecs stood waiting in a rough circle, facing out, with atlatls raised to launch the deadly spears. Two slings whirred through the air at half speed. Long minutes passed as they strained to spot the danger that they knew was present. Then, without a sound, from behind trees and bushes 15 men materialized, completely surrounding the camp! Each had a bow at full draw, arrow locked on one of the standing figures.

In dead silence the two groups stared at each other. The attackers had streaks of colored paint slashed across their faces. A few wore only loincloths, the rest were dressed in cloth shirts and pants with a sash around the waist like the Aztecs. All wore knee-high moccasins and headbands. There was an odd similarity between them and the little band facing them, despite their murderous intent.

After a minute or so, when no arrows were fired, Cuto spoke in a low, clear voice to his men. "Lower your weapons slowly. If they had wanted to fire, we would all be dead by now."

The atlatls were slowly brought down and the singing of the slings ceased as husband and wife lowered them to the ground. Cuto's observation was accurate, it seemed as though the invaders were uncertain about what to do. They didn't relax their posture and the arrows remained notched, bows bent. One of them, slightly taller than the rest, had a single feather extending from the back of his headband. Cuto guessed that this was the leader and directed his gaze at him. He knew their fate rested on this man's decision.

CHAPTER 17
Surprise

At the sound of Cuto's voice, Swallow had rolled over and sat up, rubbing her eyes. The sudden movement caused two bows to swivel toward her and, with a little cry, she ran to Ria and clung to her. Another minute passed while Indians and Aztecs studied each other.

Sudden movement from Swallow, who had been staring fixedly at the leader, broke the stalemate. With a shout she wrenched free from Ria and ran straight at him! He immediately directed his arrow at her but still didn't release the bowstring. As the Aztecs watched in astonishment, he abruptly released the tension on the bow and dropped to one knee, holding arms wide toward the running girl. She raced into his arms and embraced him with all her strength! For an instant he pushed her back and studied her face before hugging her to his chest again and calling out a single word to his men. A murmur went through the ranks but not a weapon was lowered.

After a moment, Swallow pulled back and began speaking rapidly to the man in a strange language, pointing to Cuto and Ria. Another word rang out from the leader and tension was released on the bow strings and arrows replaced in quivers. Swallow broke away and ran to the Aztec couple. Grabbing them by the hands, she pulled them to the leader who gripped Cuto's right forearm with his hand, a universal sign of friendship, and smiled broadly!

Cuto returned the clasp, still in bewilderment about what had happened. Finally he stepped to the supplies and laid out two blankets, gesturing for the other to join him at the campfire. While Ria and the others lit the fire and cut great slices of meat from the pig carcass, Swallow led the tall man to the blankets where he and Cuto sat facing each other and began to talk with their hands. The 14 other Indians sat in a semicircle behind their leader.

"I am Swallow's father," signed the man. "Two years ago she was taken from us by raiding Comanche. We never thought to see her again but she has told me about her escape and how you have cared for her. We are seeking soldiers and I thought we had found them when we approached your camp, but it is clear that you are neither soldiers, nor a war party, and I hesitated to attack because we are not a warlike people. In that moment, Swallow woke and recognized me."

"A good thing for us!" Cuto's hands replied. "But why do you seek soldiers with the intent to kill?"

"Two of our women disappeared 14 days ago while walking to the soldier's town. We found their bodies in the desert several days later and the tracks showed it was conquistadors that murdered them. We believe they are deserters because the trail shows eight men on foot leaving Santa Fe. Normal patrols are larger and have one or two leaders mounted on horses. These men are using ravines and streambeds to hide from sight as they head south; a sure sign of deserters."

"Is there anything unusual about the tracks?"

The warrior glanced sharply at him before replying. "Yes, one of them has a deformed left foot which drags as he walks."

Cuto smiled broadly. "You need search no more! Your quest is over." With flying fingers he described their encounter with the renegades. Grunts of approval rang out from the men behind as they read his hands.

A happy grin split the face of the leader. "We are Pueblo Indians, now twice in debt to you. You rescued Swallow and you have avenged the deaths of our women. I extend the hospitality of our pueblo for as long as you visit this land. You have honored us in a way that we can never repay!" He nodded at the fire. "We have meat and corn in our packs to share, let us eat together!"

CHAPTER 18

Allies

Once the Pueblo men realized that Cuto and his band were actually allies, all signs of animosity evaporated and they mingled freely with the Aztecs, hands talking busily. Hunters slipped away along the river, more campfires were started, and the morning air was soon filled with delicious aromas as food was prepared.

The atlatls and the slings fascinated the Indians, who had never seen anything like them. After eating, Cuto obliged them by demonstrating his weapon, while the other men threw spear after spear into small targets with pinpoint accuracy. The warriors, of course, wanted to try the sling and atlatl for themselves. The throwing sticks were not too different from launching a spear by hand and they caught on quickly enough, although accuracy was sadly lacking. The sling, however, was a different matter! Rocks flew through the air in every direction, to the accompaniment of uproarious laughter, as one Pueblo after another attempted the device. Errant missiles scattered the onlookers frequently and one brave caused everyone to roll on the ground, convulsed with laughter, when the sling somehow wrapped itself around his neck and blacked his eye with the still loaded pouch!

Although capable on the warpath, the Pueblos were farmers similar to the Aztec. The sacks of dried corn and seeds carried by the donkeys were of great interest to them but they found sign language too limited to convey matters of agriculture. Both sides had to wait until there was verbal communication; although the Aztecs got the idea that their new friends had some interesting farming techniques to show them.

Cuto pressed Swallow's father, whose name was Feather, about Santa Fe.

"We have heard there are many soldiers in the town and supplies often run short. Do you trade food to them? Some say they are a hard people."

Feather nodded. "In the early years, they easily crushed all resistance because of their horses. Even warlike people like the Comanche, Kiowa, and Apache had no chance against mounted men. Everyone learned to stay away or submit to them. Gradually the Pueblo have been able to develop trade but the conquistadors are still unpredictable and dangerous. We only allow the older men and women to take vegetables and fruit to town because our young men cannot control their tempers and the young women or children are subject to being taken as slaves."

"Why do your people take such a risk?"

"There are other men in Santa Fe these days, the 'men in black.' They are gentle, carry no weapons, and seem interested in getting to know us. They appear to have some influence on how we are treated by the soldiers. Also, the conquistadors have excellent trade goods: cloth, beads, cooking utensils, and tools. We make good use of such things for ourselves or to trade with other Indians. Since the conquistadors are always hungry, and we are farmers, the proposition is a good one."

Cuto, the hunter, had a final question. "What about meat?"

"Wild game is an excellent trade item. They have chickens and pigs but most of the meat comes salted in barrels and they tire of it quickly." Feather gave him an appraising look. "They would welcome a good hunter. But their arrogance must not be allowed to goad one into losing his temper!"

Mulling over the conversation, and remembering Coyotl's remark about how they would have fared if the renegades had been mounted, an idea began to stir in Cuto's brain. If the Indians had horses…

The following day, the whole party left the river and set out on a more direct line to the Indian pueblo. They traveled leisurely through the desert that still sported patches of flowers, boldly painting the landscape until the heat of summer would dry them up. The Indians were familiar with every source of water and each night they camped at small springs with ample grass for the donkeys. In the evenings, brilliant sunsets set scattered clouds ablaze with orange.

Four days later they approached a large structure built against the side of a steep hill. Three things struck the Aztecs, who had never seen anything but small single story whitewashed houses. First, the structure was huge: three stories high, 150 feet long, with two short wings extending forward at either end to form sort of a plaza in front. Second, there were no doorways at ground level; ladders accessed the second and third stories, both of which had openings to inner rooms. Third, the entire building was pale blue!

Anasazi

"Blue?" Sophia was astonished.

Great Grandfather stood up, the story was over for another week, but she was captivated by the image of a blue building.

"Yes. Didn't you know that pueblo builders often painted their buildings? Blue, green, even pink!"

"I've never heard that," she replied.

"How did they build such a large structure and why were there no doors at ground level?" The building fascinated Juan.

"By this time the peoples in the southwest had been skilled builders for centuries, using adobe because they didn't have the unlimited supply of rock enjoyed by the Incans. A pueblo was constructed in the form of boxes, stacked on top of one another, each level being slightly smaller than the one below to allow room for walking around the outside. I imagine you can figure out the reason for the lack of doorways at the ground level." The old man raised his eyebrows.

"Defense." The boy said without hesitation.

"Of course. Pull up the ladders and the enemy is at an immediate disadvantage. Holes in the roof, and interior ladders, allowed them full use of the ground floor." He nodded toward Sophia. "The buildings were often stuccoed with sand, lime, and oyster shells."

"Wow, oyster shells! They had to come from the coastlines. That speaks to the extensive commerce throughout the Americas you've described."

"Exactly. I knew the two you have been to Mesa Verde to see the cliff dwellings, but have you heard of Chaco Canyon? It's quite an example of the ancient people's engineering sophistication."

"The name sounds familiar, we probably heard it at school."

"It's a canyon in northwestern New Mexico. Its elevation is about 6,000 feet and the topography is high desert: hot in summer and bitter cold in winter. Although there is evidence of people having lived in that area for almost 3,000 years, a great period of development began about 1,100 years ago, around 850 AD. Stone buildings were built, as high as five stories, containing hundreds of rooms! Modern archeologists call them 'great houses.' The builders used some 200,000 wood beams in the construction, brought in from mountains many miles away! There are remains of nearly 180 miles of road in the canyon and surrounding areas; roads that are wide and amazingly straight. Like the Incans, these people resorted to staircases when confronted with an obstacle to the road such as a mesa. The culture existed for almost 300 years until, most likely, a drought drove the people away."

The twins were stunned.

"200,000 beams?" Juan exclaimed.

"Yes. Possibly brought in over some of the roads, although there is confusion about what the roads were actually used for. Some seem to dead end in the desert where there is no evidence of a community. Others end pointed at what appear to be shrines or observatories. Still others seem to point from one great house to another, but don't connect the two. Despite our lack of understanding about use, the precision and skill of the road construction is undisputed."

He went on. "For the next few hundred years people in that part of the country built housing in a variety ways, ranging from great houses to cliff dwellings like those at Mesa Verde. A general term for those population groups is 'Anasazi,' which in Navajo means 'ancient ones.' Well before Cuto and Ria arrived, however, people had divided into individual tribes or cultural groups. Feather's people were part of a much larger community known by then, of course, as the Pueblo Indians."

C H A P T E R   2 0

Homecoming

WHEN THEY WERE a quarter of a mile away from the pueblo, Swallow suddenly broke loose and ran ahead as fast as she could on her bandaged feet. As she drew close to the building, people on the ground stopped what they were doing to watch her approach. When she headed for a ladder with the clear intention of climbing it, a nearby woman reached out to grab her. Without slowing, the girl turned her head toward the woman, apparently addressing her. The Indian took two steps backward, throwing a hand to her mouth in surprise, and rushed toward a group standing nearby. They all turned to watch Swallow fly up the ladder to the second level, immediately climb another to the third level, and disappear through a doorway.

"She seeks her mother," signed Feather.

Cuto and Ria nodded their understanding, eyes on the building. By now, those on the ground had spotted the returning war party and hurried to greet it with excited cries. Children dashed ahead, laughing excitedly and vying to be the first one swept up in the arms of a father. Wives, always worried that their husbands might not return, sighed with relief when they saw no one missing. As they drew close, people began emerging from the upper levels of the building smiling and waving at the scene below before starting down ladders to join the crowd. On the third story a woman stood with one arm wrapped tightly around Swallow and the other waving at Feather, her face lit up in a smile. It was a joyous time.

A large fire was built on the ground in front of the pueblo and food gathered from communal storerooms. Feasting and dancing continued well into the night as the village celebrated the recovery of Swallow and the safe return of the war party. The Aztecs were seated in places of honor on either side of Feather and his wife Dawn; Swallow was called on time and again to describe her escape from the Comanche. When she recounted being beaten and bludgeoned with the rock there were murmurs of anger. Cries of approval rang out as, with shining eyes on Ria, she described being found and nursed to health; however, dead silence reigned as the Indians listened to Feather relate the battle between the Aztecs and the renegade soldiers, confirming their identity as the missing women's murderers. As he finished, the men uttered grunts of approval and every eye was directed at the guests in appreciation.

At last the fire burned down and people began drifting to the building, some with sleeping children in their arms. Cuto and his party were shown to rooms on the third level, near to Swallow's parents. For the first time in weeks they would be sleeping indoors!

CHAPTER 21

Horses

Driven by curiosity to see Santa Fe and observe the horses, three days later Cuto persuaded Feather to take him to the outpost. They left Ria and the others at the pueblo, despite their objections.

Feather was adamant with his new friend. "Under no circumstances can your wife be allowed in the town and your young companions may not be able to control themselves if provoked. The soldiers are bored and look for any opportunity to take out their frustrations. You must agree to remain quiet and appear submissive at all times."

"I will do as you say," replied Cuto's fingers. He thought it better not to mention the sling wrapped around his waist.

Arriving in the late afternoon, they passed adobe houses scattered along the banks of a stream and approached the center of the community: a large dirt square completely enclosed by low buildings. A 50-foot gap between two of the buildings provided entry to the area, which measured 100 yards square. As they entered, Cuto saw that the building across the plaza had many doorways. He stopped to stare, never had he seen so many doors!

"That's where the Spanish leaders conduct the business of ruling this region, which they call 'New Mexico,'" the Pueblo signed, noticing his friend's astonishment. "Other buildings are for soldiers and the holy men who dress in black."

Feather had casually stopped just inside the opening, the blanket around his shoulders apparently for warmth against the coming night's chill but drawn in such a way to hide his flying fingers. It was better that the soldiers not understand that a stranger had entered the plaza.

In the middle of the square, 15 older Indian men and women sat on blankets, a variety of food items displayed in front of them. A few soldiers, and one of the men in black, moved slowly among them, occasionally exchanging a trinket or bit of colorful cloth for food.

Off duty soldiers lounged on long benches in front of the building to the left, talking and laughing among themselves. Only one, a smallish man leaning against a barracks door jam, appeared to take any notice of them. He had a pointed black beard and narrow set eyes; a sword hung in a scabbard at his hip. His eyes locked on the two and never wavered.

The medallion was warm against Cuto's chest, but did not get hot; clearly there was danger, but it didn't seem imminent. To the right, at the far corner of the square, there was a fenced area containing a number of horses. Cuto spied them and his eyes widened. He used his own blanket for hiding his hands; to a casual observer, they were just two Indians observing the traders.

"Are those animals the horses about which you speak?"

"Yes, some are kept inside the square and others nearby in an enclosure along the stream. They are closely guarded day and night."

"They are much larger than I imagined." Cuto marveled to himself. He realized why the soldiers had such an advantage in battle. Mounted on animals like these, they would be nearly invincible. On the other hand, mounted Indians would be more than a match for them!

"Watch that one!" With an almost imperceptible move of his head, Feather directed the Aztec's attention to the man staring at them. "He has whipped and beaten many of my people for no reason other than looking him in the eye. He hates all Indians and makes no attempt to hide it. We should go now."

Even as the two men turned away, one of the soldiers suddenly rose and gave a shout, pointing at the entrance. The trading was over for the day. The Indians immediately began loading their goods into sacks and folding up the blankets; within minutes they were walking out into the village.

"No one is allowed inside the square at night." Feather explained.

Cuto nodded, but he had seen all that he needed to see.

CHAPTER 22

Palace of Governors

UNABLE TO CONTAIN his curiosity, Juan interrupted. "Excuse me Great Grandfather, but the square and that building with all the doors. That sounds like the Plaza and The Palace of Governors in Santa Fe that we visited last year with Mom and Dad."

"That's exactly what it was." The old man smiled.

"But I thought Santa Fe would be sort of a fort when Cuto and Ria arrived; an outpost for the Spaniards, with nothing around."

"Actually, Santa Fe is the oldest surviving capital city in the country and perhaps the third oldest city established by Europeans. St. Augustine, Florida is the oldest, founded in 1565, while Jamestown, Virginia was also founded in 1607.

"There is evidence that Pueblo Indians were living in what is now the vicinity of the Plaza as early as 1050 AD. The Santa Fe River provided water, although it is an endangered river now; by the time the Spaniards arrived in 1598 the community was well established. The newcomers first created their headquarters at what we know as Espanola, just to the north, to manage the vast lands in the Southwest they laid claim to. In 1607, the Spanish leader, Don Pedro de Peralta, moved the headquarters to what is now the Plaza of modern Santa Fe. He proclaimed the town to be the capital of the province. Around 1610 he built the Palace of the Governors. Cuto and Ria probably arrived in the spring of 1611, so the description passed down to us is most likely accurate."

"Feather said that the conquistadors were hard on the Indians," interjected Sophia.

"There is no question about it," Great Grandfather nodded. "The Indians were conscripted as workers to construct buildings, defense walls, etc., and were treated poorly from the beginning. For a while Don Peralta tried to improve their condition by disciplining soldiers guilty of abusing Indians, but subsequent leaders were not so conscientious. Conditions gradually deteriorated until it all came to a head in 1680." He paused, grinning. "But that's another story."

CHAPTER 23

Canyon

FEATHER'S COMMUNITY numbered 200 men, women, and children. Most of them climbed daily to work gardens on top of the steep mesa behind the building. The Aztecs were amazed because, unlike their home far to the south, there was no river to supply irrigation water. Mesa tops normally featured an inhospitable planting environment due to large expanses of bare rock interspersed with patches of rocky soil. They were therefore astonished to discover more than two acres of greenery standing in stark contrast to the dry surroundings!

Their hosts proudly showed them large catch basins, cut in solid rock, for capturing rainwater.

Several feet deep and many yards across, the basins were connected to each other, and to the gardens, by a cleverly designed system of canals. Water was released by lifting blocks of rock that dammed the basins.

"We can go for many weeks without rain," Feather explained. "If the basins get low, we carry water to them from our drinking spring at the bottom of the hill."

The visitors quickly fit into pueblo life. They were given several garden plots and planted a variety of beans and other vegetables with seeds carried from home. While the Indians had some crops that the newcomers were unfamiliar with, the latter grew avocados and varieties of hot peppers that the Pueblo had not tasted, so each learned from the other. The language barrier was soon overcome and farming topics consumed evening conversations.

Cuto resumed his habit of hunting and, before long deer, rabbit, quail, javelina, and desert sheep became a regular part of the pueblo diet. Following Adzul's example, he made a practice of delivering choice cuts to the aged and infirm, all of whom looked forward to his visits. He particularly liked stalking the wary sheep in rocky hills scattered throughout the region and would sometimes stay out for several days. Ria frequently joined him on the hunts usually accompanied by Swallow, who had become like a shadow to her. It was on one of these expeditions that the Indian girl disappeared.

They had been away for two nights and were many miles east of the pueblo, hunting along a dry wash. Swallow had been learning the sling and had spent the last hour stalking an elusive jackrabbit. When it finally stopped long enough for her to throw, the rock literally flew between its ears and the rabbit disappeared for good into a crevice.

"You almost took off one of its ears!" Ria encouraged the crestfallen girl. "Keep practicing, you've shown wonderful improvement for the short time you've been at it!"

Since evening was coming on, they began searching for a spring. Swallow suddenly stopped and swung her head from one side to the other, searching the terrain.

"I know where we are," she announced. "Follow me."

She set off at a rapid pace and 20 minutes later arrived on the rim of a huge canyon cut in the desert floor, running south to north. They stared down steep cliffs at a grassy valley 300 feet below, highlighted by a shimmering creek. A quarter of a mile away, matching red cliffs rose back up to the desert floor, awash with color from the setting sun.

"It's beautiful." Ria murmured, unable to pull her eyes away from the stunning scene.

"My father used to bring me here when I was small."

The girl turned to the right and led the way along the rim for almost 100 yards. She seemed to be studying the ground. Suddenly she knelt with her back to the canyon and pointed with one arm to the desert.

"Did you see that? Was it a jaguar?" she cried.

Cuto and Ria whirled to stare through the fading light in the direction she pointed. For minutes their eyes searched every cactus and bit of rock in sight.

"Where was it?" Cuto spoke softly.

There was no reply. Repeating the question he turned toward the girl, but she was gone!

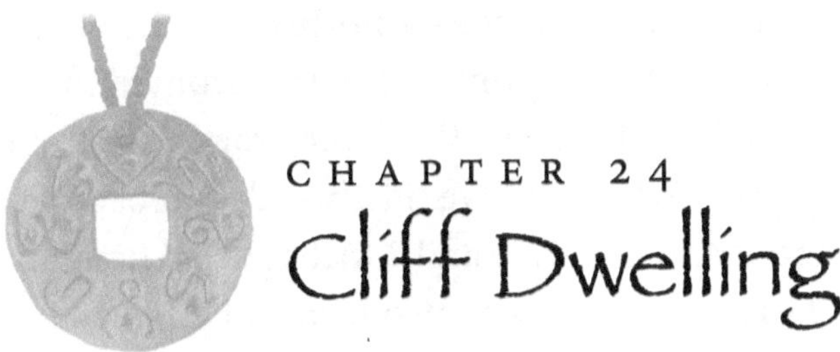# CHAPTER 24
Cliff Dwelling

THE COUPLE STEPPED over to the rim and peered down. The rock sloped gradually for 10 feet and then dropped straight down; they could see nothing below the rounded edge.

"She couldn't have fallen," said Ria. "She would have called out."

They stared at each other, wondering what possibly could have happened.

"Are you looking for me?" The words were accompanied by a giggle and seemed surprisingly close.

"Where are you?" Ria leaned out as far as she dared but couldn't see anything.

"Down here. I wasn't sure if I would remember after all these years."

"Remember what?" Cuto was confused.

"The handholds. Look at your feet."

For a moment they saw nothing on the rock beneath them. Then it jumped out: two grooves cut in the surface 10 inches down the sloping rock slope from where they stood! They were side-by-side, a foot apart, each about 4 inches wide and 2 inches deep. Roughly 18 inches below them were two identical grooves.

"I see four cuts in the rock," he announced.

"Yes, they're for climbing down," came the words from below. "This is important: Put your right hand in the left higher groove and your right foot in the left lower cut, ignore the holes to the right. Slide your left foot down the rock and it will come to a hole on the left that you can't see, and then slide your right foot down to the left groove that you can see. For the first move only your right hand will have a hold; after that the holes are off set so you will always have good handholds when you stretch a foot down to the next hole."

"Why not use the two grooves on the right to start?" Cuto questioned.

"It's a trap. I'll explain later."

Husband and wife stared at each other. As far as they could tell, below the rounded edge, the cliff was nearly sheer all the way to the bottom. Only the girl's voice from beneath gave them confidence that the cuts in the rock would actually allow them to descend.

"I'll go first." Cuto declared, uncertain about what lay below.

He slipped off his sandals, to better grip the rock with his toes, and started down. The hand and footholds were exactly where Swallow had described, but when he moved over the rounded section the cliff went straight down and there was nothing but air between his feet and a jumble of boulders far below. Although the grooves were perfectly positioned, and deep enough to create stability, he was unable to tear his eyes from the immense drop beneath him and froze.

"Don't look down," Swallow's calm voice rose through the air. "Look at the rock directly in front of you and feel for the footholds."

Forcing himself to follow her instructions, the Aztec focused on the rock surface 10 inches from his face, seeing small bumps worn almost smooth by wind and rain. Gradually his breathing slowed and the rigid muscles in his arms and legs relaxed.

"We're like flyspecks on this cliff," he muttered under his breath. "If I slip..."

Freeing a foot from the safety of its hole and sliding it down the rock to the next groove was one of the hardest things he had ever done. Just as he was starting to panic and draw his foot back, the toes slid into the opening below and he was secure. Bit by bit, he made his way slowly down, finding that Swallow's advice worked; as long as he didn't look down, the descent was manageable. Glancing up, he saw Ria smoothly following; she had heard the instructions and her face was firmly directed at the rock in front of her.

After descending 150 feet he found a grinning Swallow standing on a ledge to his right. "I've found something as difficult for you as the sling is for me. 'It just takes practice,'" she chortled, echoing one of his favorite expressions.

"You might have warned me about not looking down!" Cuto glared at her in feigned anger, amazed that this slip of a girl could handle the gradient so easily.

Ria arrived a minute later and they followed Swallow along the ledge for a few yards until, rounding a corner, they stopped in amazement. There in the face of the cliff was an enormous cave! It was at least 40 feet high and 200 feet long, and extended 60 feet back into the rock. In it had been built a three-level complex of rooms that looked like a small version of the pueblo, even to the remnants of ladders still leaning against the walls. Cuto judged it to be 100 feet above the valley floor.

"Who built this?" Ria's voice was hushed, as though they were intruding on forbidden ground.

"The Ancient Ones," replied the girl. "They lived here long ago and designed their home for defense. The handholds are the only access from above or below and are so designed that you must start with hands and feet in the proper holes or you will reach a point where you cannot continue! That's why I warned you to ignore the first two grooves on the right. If you hadn't, when you reached the little knob up there that almost touches your stomach, your arms and legs would have become crossed and prevented you from going further without starting over. In the meantime, you would be exposed to arrows shot from the ledge."

Cuto grunted in appreciation of the ingenuity. He remembered the rounded spot she described. "How many sets of handholds are there?"

"There are two sets off the rim and four coming up from below. Most of the travel was down to the valley because they farmed along the stream; the outlines of the gardens are still visible."

The ledge passed along the bottom of the cliff dwelling and Swallow led the way to what was clearly a newer ladder reaching to the second level.

"My father built this ladder, and the one above, some years ago," she explained. "At that time the Comanche were attacking constantly and he thought about moving our people here. It would be easier to defend than the pueblo and there is even a small spring coming out of the rock, so he could have held out for a long time. For some reason the raids tapered off, so we never moved."

She led the way along the second level to a room her father had cleaned out for them to use in the past. There was a small fireplace cleverly built into one back corner and a pile of wood left from Feather's last visit. After building a fire, they broke out jerky and dried corn from their provisions and spent a comfortable night protected from the desert chill.

The climb back to the rim was noticeably easier the following morning and Cuto was reminded of Swallow's words about practice. As they headed across the desert toward the pueblo, he realized the canyon dropped so abruptly into the desert floor that it was invisible from less than a half mile away. He wondered whether the Spaniards even knew it existed.

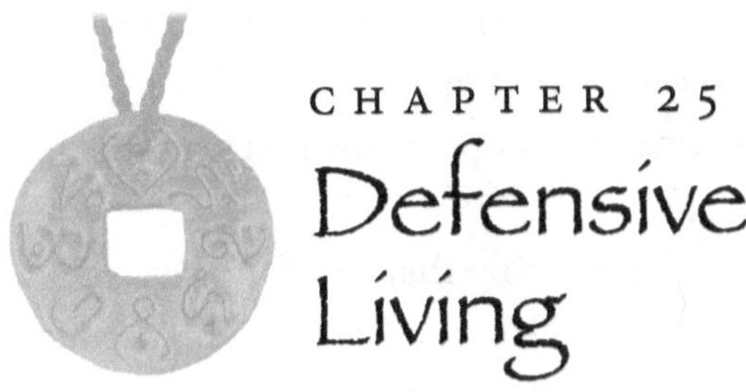

CHAPTER 25

Defensive Living

"ONE HUNDRED AND FIFTY FEET! That's about 15 stories!" Juan was incredulous. "Imagine looking off the top of a building that high and trying to climb down, using small footholds and no rope!"

"Along with the risk of getting stuck halfway down and having arrows shot at you," Great Grandfather added.

"Did kids go up and down?" Sophia was horrified at the idea.

"Probably not little kids; they would have been carried. But as soon as they could reach the holes, I'm sure no one could stop them."

"That's so dangerous! What if they fell?"

"If it was the cliff dwelling that Cuto and Ria were in, anyone that fell would not have survived. But not all cliff houses had sheer walls above and below for 150 feet. Many of them had rocky slopes coming up to the bottom of the houses, or a short section of broken cliffs below the lowest level of rooms."

"I just can't imagine people living that way." Sophia was still skeptical.

"People have been living that way for centuries all over the world," Great Grandfather smiled. "Sixteen hundred years ago Buddhist monks in India built a series of homes in the side of a cliff that are called the Ajanta Caves: they ranged from 35 to 110 feet above the river below. The monks used ladders to reach them.

"In Mali, a republic in northwest Africa, there's a 90 mile-long section of rock face called the Bandiagara Escarpment. An ancient people called the Tellem lived in homes built on cliffs that are 1500 feet high. Some of the dwellings can still be seen today.

"In Israel there are the ruins of a fortress called Masada. It sits on a plateau that has cliffs ranging from 300 to 1300 feet high. After the sack of Jerusalem in 70 AD, a group of militant refugees settled there. The access to the top is extremely difficult and when the Romans mounted an expedition against them in 73 AD, they had to build a 375-foot high ramp of rock and dirt to attack!"

"Wow!" Juan was always interested in the military side of things. "What happened?"

"The Romans won, as they usually did in those days," replied the old man. He turned back to Sophia. "When people chose to live in or on cliffs as a defense against enemies, their children had to climb. In fact, they were probably better at it than a lot of adults. Children climb like monkeys!"

The twins laughed.

"You're right," Juan exclaimed. "I've seen kids make outrageous moves on the climbing wall at school. Come to think of it, Sophia was one of them!"

"Well, that's different." His sister muttered.

"Point well made." Great Grandfather grinned.

CHAPTER 26

Capture

Unable to get horses out of his mind, Cuto slipped away to Santa Fe a month later to reconnoiter the corrals. This time he strolled around the outside of the walled plaza until he spotted 30 of the animals in a fenced area along the stream. Eight soldiers were spread evenly along the perimeter of the small pasture, so he stopped 50 yards away to observe the horses. As he stood there, stories from his grandfather came to mind about how horses had turned the tide of battle against both Incan and Aztec armies. The warriors on foot had been both intimidated by the animals and outclassed by their speed and maneuverability. It had taken years to develop bolas and other defense

intent in the eyes of the approaching soldier. For a fleeting second he regretted not having put on the armor shirt that morning; it would momentarily have made a fool out of the conquistador if he aimed his killing thrust at the heart. Overriding that thought, however, was a great sadness that he had failed Adzul through his impetuous action in coming alone to see the horses. Feather would never have let him get so close to them.

Although the medallion was hidden beneath the shirt, upon his death it would fall into the hands of the Spaniards—the very people Adzul had risked his life to keep it from. Shame filled him for betraying the trust of the old warrior. The best he could do was to die with honor, as his great grandfather Qist had; he vowed to himself that not a sound would pass his lips, no matter what happened.

"Slowly, he must die slowly," the Lieutenant thought with pleasure. "I will make an example of him that the traders will never forget!"

He walked up to the bound man, slowly raising the razor sharp blade toward his face. A flick of the wrist would take off the nose; perhaps the ears would follow before he got to the eyes. Though beaten and bloody, he had a fearless look that infuriated the soldier and he swore the Indian would scream for mercy before he died! The deadly steel caressed Cuto's left cheek.

"Perhaps the man has been disciplined enough, Lieutenant."

The soldier turned, lowering his blade. Behind him stood a large man in black robes. A full beard, streaked with gray, covered his chest and kindly brown eyes looked out from a weathered face. It was Father Montoya, a Franciscan friar, and Head of the Church in New Mexico.

"Father Montoya, I thought you were visiting Taos Pueblo," the lieutenant bowed his head to hide his anger. The Father was the most powerful man in the province and the only man he feared more than the Commander. Even his father's great wealth could not influence the friar.

"I returned this morning," replied the older man. "What has this man done that merits approaching him with a naked sword?" The friar's voice was gentle but his eyes were direct and unwavering.

"He was trying to steal horses and he attacked one of the soldiers."

"I heard that he had only approached the horses too closely and pushed when one of the men grabbed him from behind." The voice was mild but firm. "I suggest we ask the Commandant about the proper discipline."

"As you wish, Father." Marquez reluctantly sheathed the sword and they strode together toward the administrative building.

Cuto watched them go, remembering Feather's words that the men in black were friendlier than the soldiers. But for the big man's intervention, he knew he would have been tortured to death…he had seen Marquez's look. He thought of the murdered Pueblo women and remembered how the deserting renegades had stared at Ria. A great anger began to flood through him at the arrogance of those with military superiority. They had to be stopped.

CHAPTER 27
Torture

The influence of Father Montoya was such that he was received immediately by the commanding officer, Colonel Rodriguez. He and the friar sat at a table, with Marquez standing behind them, while soldiers from the pasture were called to describe the incident. Intimidated by the presence of the Holy Father, the men dared not lie and reported the events accurately; even admitting that weeks of boredom had probably caused them to overreact. The questioning over, Rodriguez turned to the lieutenant. He saw the anger smoldering in those black eyes and thought of Marquez's repeated bullying of the Indians. His voice took on an edge.

"As you know, Lieutenant, I am trying to gain the friendship of these Indians. They greatly outnumber us and an uprising could be dangerous. Only the horses would give us a chance to survive. According to Father Montoya, the man has already been severely beaten. I think the punishment is sufficient. Lock him in the empty storeroom at the end of this building for three days, providing water only. After that he is to be released with orders never to go near the horses again, on pain of death."

"Yes sir." Marquez kept his voice steady as he spun on his heel and left the room seething with rage. He mentally denounced Rodriguez as a coward, the Indians understood only one thing: force. A plan began to take root in his brain. In two days the friar was scheduled to leave for Sandia Pueblo. With him gone, there would still be time to make an example of the Indian.

Returning to the square, Marquez made a great show of removing the rope from around Cuto's neck and retying his wrists in front of him so that he could manage a drinking gourd. He then had one of the soldiers escort the captive to the storeroom. Another soldier was directed to bring a bucket of water and gourd for the prisoner and the lieutenant made a point of taking the bucket to the storeroom. No one saw him kick it over just before closing the door.

When Father Montoya left on the afternoon of the second day, the lieutenant smiled with satisfaction, knowing he wouldn't return for a week. He would make the captive pay dearly that very night for the insolent look in his eyes. The next morning, with all the traders as witnesses, Marquez would escort the prisoner out of the square, wrapped in a blanket to hide his wounds. No one could say that the Commander's orders had not been followed, nor would they see the Lieutenant himself escort the prisoner far into the desert and torture him to the point of death, leaving the broken body for vultures and coyotes to finish.

The hot medallion woke Cuto in the middle of the night. Soft footsteps approached and he heard the storeroom door open and close as someone entered the room. Light flickered as a candle was lit and he saw the man who had wanted to kill him; who kicked over the water bucket every day so that a raging thirst now burned his parched mouth and throat. The candle was set on the floor and the man came toward him, smiling. Unable to resist because of the ropes around his ankles and wrists, the Aztec could only struggle helplessly as he was lifted and hung by the wrists from a heavy nail high in the wall, his toes just touching the floor.

Dangling, with his face to the wall, Cuto heard the rustle of cloth as the lieutenant moved back to the candle and took off his coat. There was a soft laugh just before the first lash of the heavy whip struck like a knife, tearing his shirt and leaving an open wound in his back. The heavy braided leather, knotted at the end, bit into him time after time, tearing clothes and biting deeply into flesh with every stroke. Red mist swam before Cuto's eyes but not a sound escaped his clenched teeth. Infuriated that the victim uttered no cry, Marquez put all his force into each stroke until, after 30 minutes, he ran out of strength. By then the warrior was unconscious, torn and bloody from shoulders to knees. Soaked in sweat, the soldier shrugged into his coat and blew out the candle. With another soft chuckle, he stepped outside and returned to his quarters.

CHAPTER 28

Rescue

Two hours before dawn there was a faint scratching sound on the ceiling of the storeroom. Bits of straw and adobe began falling to the floor as a small opening was hacked in the roof.

"Cuto?" A voice whispered. "Cuto, we've come to get you; Ria and your men are with Father on the roof."

There was no sound from the figure hanging on the wall. More scratching followed and soon a larger hole was opened to the night sky.

"I'm certain this is the room Raven Wing described but maybe they moved him," Feather whispered in Swallow's ear. "The hole's big enough for us to lower you down. See if he's there."

In a minute the girl was on the floor. The room was pitch black except for a dim radiance from the stars filtering through the hole.

"Cuto?" she whispered. Then more sharply "Cuto!"

A shuddering groan to her left broke the stillness and she suddenly became aware of blood smell. Hands outstretched, the girl took step after step in the direction of the sound until her fingers brushed a body. At the touch, another soft groan emerged out of the dark. Within seconds the light touch of her fingers told the story.

She hissed at the opening. "Father, you've got to get down here! He's tied to the wall and badly hurt!"

Within minutes the hole in the ceiling had been enlarged yet again and a figure dropped to the floor.

"Here," Swallow directed. "He's tied up and hanging by his arms. Be careful of his back."

She guided her father's hands to the body and in another minute his knife had cut the ropes and the Aztec was lowered to the floor. Each movement elicited a soft moan from the now semi-conscious man. A series of hurried whisperings took place between Feather and the men on the roof; a loop of the leather line was lowered and placed under the wounded man's arms. Mercifully, as the rope tightened on his savaged back, he passed out. Mazatl and Tenoch were on the other end of the rope, surrounded by several Pueblo warriors with bows at the ready.

As gently as possible Cuto was pulled out and carried to the back of the building where he was lowered to Coyotl, Xpil, Ria, and three more Pueblo warriors. His wife let out a soft moan as the unconscious body, reeking of blood, was placed over Patli's shoulder in a sort of fireman's carry. She grabbed one of her husband's limp hands but there was no response. They immediately set out for the desert, guided by the Indians, leaving the two Aztec men to wait for the others on the roof. Less than 15 minutes after the rescue team's arrival at the back of the plaza, all had melted away into the shadows.

CHAPTER 29

Bullying

"BULLY!" SOPHIA INTERRUPTED spitting out the word. "Just like those high school kids who threatened Juan's team after the tournament. That man was nothing but a bully protected by his father!"

"Worse than that," said her brother. "Given the chance, he would have tortured and killed Cuto right in the square."

Great Grandfather nodded. "Throughout history victorious armies have inflicted enormous pain on the peoples they conquered. The siege of Jerusalem by Romans in 70 AD resulted in more than 1,000,000 men, women, and children being killed in less than four months! The historian Josephus reported the

Roman soldiers were so carried away that, at the end, they simply had nothing left to kill!

"For 300 years the Barbary Coast pirates raided the ships and coastal towns of Europe, capturing and selling more than 1,250,000 men, women, and children into slavery in North Africa. Just imagine the suffering and hardship it caused! It only stopped when the great sea powers, including the United States of America, had had enough and broke them in the early 1800s.

"Brutality is just an extension of bullying. In modern times countless people, including children, have been killed. The Holocaust is one and the reign of terror in Russia by Stalin, another.

"Whether it's kids, adults, or armies, when one loses compassion and sensitivity for others, bullying becomes all too easy."

"Remember the time in fourth grade when Sophia got a black eye for standing up to defend that girl with a stutter?" Juan grinned. "She took on a kid who out-weighed her by 40 pounds and was a head taller! I didn't even have to step in; she had that girl on the ground begging for mercy by the time the playground supervisor broke it up! No one ever teased the stutterer again!"

Sophia's eyes flashed as she remembered the incident. "Julia overcame the stutter and turned out to be one of the best students in the class. She became one of my closest friends until she moved away to Denver."

"I'm not surprised," said the old man. "Doing the right thing doesn't always have such noticeable results, but it does give you peace of mind. Unfortunately, the object of the bullying pays a price; Cuto's scars would be with him for the rest of his life."

CHAPTER 30

Reprisal

A LAUGHING FACE accompanied the whip flashing in the air, and then searing pain dragged Cuto away from the nightmare, his breath whistling softly through clenched teeth. As consciousness flooded in, he realized that he was lying face down on soft blankets, surrounded by the familiar adobe walls of their room in the pueblo.

"He's awake!" the soft voice of his wife came from beside him as a gentle hand held his head down when he weakly tried to rise. "Stay still, my love, or you will open your wounds and start bleeding again."

Too spent to resist, and with his back feeling like it was on fire, he lay back. "What happened?" his voice grated with the pain.

"The traders got word to us of the events in the square and where you were locked up. They feared for your life when the man in black went away and sent a runner to warn us. We immediately set out with Feather and some warriors to rescue you. Swallow would not be left behind, convincing her father that she could slip through a small hole in the roof and help you escape.

"But when I got into the room you were unconscious from the whipping," Swallow's voice came from the other side of his body. "My father had to drop down with a rope to pull you out. Patli and the others took turns carrying you back to the pueblo."

"What about the medallion? Did he get it?" The Aztec weakly tried to move a hand under his chest.

"No, it's still around your neck," Ria said softly, gently restraining him. "Right where it belongs."

"For three days and nights Ria and my mother have never left your side. They have used all their skills to treat your back. One day the men who did this will pay!" Swallow's voice was tight with anger.

"But you must rest because the wounds are still fresh," interjected the voice of her mother, "and the poultices need more time."

"It was not the man in black with the kind eyes, it was the smaller one with murder in his gaze," the words trailed off as he drifted into unconsciousness.

A week after the rescue, Cuto was able to move around gingerly. His back was covered with poultices made from wild honey and herbs and wrapped in soft cloth from neck to waist and both legs were bandaged to the knees. The ghastly wounds, which had exposed parts of his ribs, were beginning to heal but motion brought shards of pain through the torn flesh so he needed no encouragement to remain still. Most days he sat cross-legged on the upper level of the pueblo watching the Indians go about their daily activities and talking with Feather or his Aztec friends.

Conversation usually turned to horses and his conviction that the animals were the key to independence. The matter of obtaining them was discussed endlessly but no one could come up with a strategy to overcome the conquistadors' extremely tight security. The solution presented itself out of the blue.

Four weeks after the rescue Cuto was beginning to resume his normal activities, although his back and legs were ugly with the angry red scars, when word came from the traders that the soldiers had discovered his whereabouts. An expedition was being organized to recapture him and apprehend those that had broken into the storeroom.

"Who supplied this information?" Cuto inquired.

"One of our old women speaks Spanish and monitors the soldiers' conversations from her blanket in the square," Feather explained. "She is small, innocuous, and arouses no suspicion; her information has always been invaluable. I'm surprised they identified our pueblo because we swept away every trace of tracks on the way home."

After the rescue the traders had made a point of coming and going from the plaza as a group, and always in broad daylight, but Marquez had finally managed to catch one of them alone. Far out in the desert, under horrible torture, he had revealed that Cuto once visited Santa Fe in the company of Feather. After killing the old man, the lieutenant reported the information to the Commander and was put in charge of the expedition to recapture the Aztec and bring in those responsible for his escape.

"Our informant says the troop will leave tomorrow in the direction of Taos Pueblo to the north, disguising its real objective. After a few miles, it will swing south around Santa Fe and arrive here in the afternoon of the third day. She warned that the leader is the one who wanted to kill you."

"This is our chance," exclaimed Cuto.

"Chance for what?" Past experience with the conquistadors caused the Indian to expect harsh reprisal against women and children in addition to his men. He knew that Marquez would have no mercy and he had been ready to order the entire village to abandon the pueblo and retreat to the desert. As the Aztec outlined his idea, however, the Indian's head began to nod in agreement, growing excitement in his eyes. "Our young men will welcome such an opportunity."

The following day all women and children left to hide in the southern hills, taking the domesticated animals. Only able-bodied men and older boys remained behind.

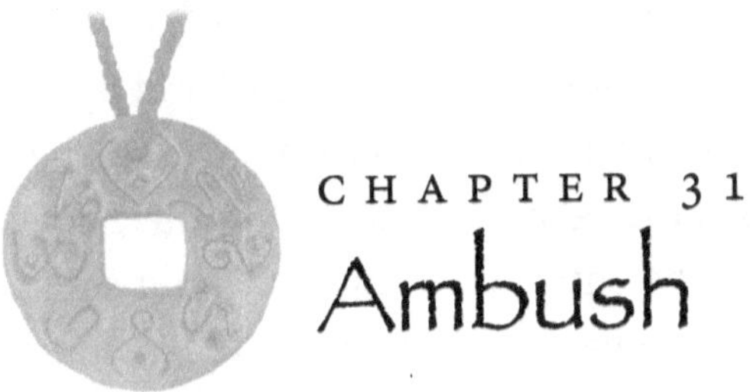

CHAPTER 31
Ambush

A CLOUD OF DUST LIFTING slowly into the sky marked the column as it neared the pueblo the next afternoon. There were 30 soldiers on foot, armed with lances and swords; eight mounted officers accompanied them, led by Lieutenant Marquez. Just outside the two short wings extending from either end of the building, the expedition stopped and spread out in a long line with the officers in front. For a few moments there was silence as they studied the situation.

Ladders leaned against all levels of the blue structure, some slightly askew as if they had been descended in great haste. Baskets and debris littered the ground in front and empty doorways gaped from every story.

There was not a person in sight. Behind the pueblo rose the contrasting red mesa with its numerous trails for gardeners to ascend. All was still except for two vultures cruising high above.

"The cockroaches have fled," muttered Marquez, muscles in his jaw bulging with rage. Ordered by the Commandant to return Cuto, and those who rescued him, to Santa Fe, the lieutenant had had other ideas. Annihilation of the entire community would set an example for every Indian in the area that the conquistadors were not to be taken lightly. He would simply report that he had been ruthlessly attacked and had to defend himself and his men. But the cowards had now foiled his plan by fleeing. The traders must have warned them; they would die when he returned to Santa Fe. Leading the way into the courtyard strewn with debris, he shouted orders.

"Climb the ladders and collect everything inside. Pack up any food and pile the rest against the walls to fire this place. I want only ashes when we leave! If you find anyone inside bring him or her to me unharmed, I will find out where the others have gone." He smiled grimly; anyone unfortunate enough to stay behind would wish they were dead before he was finished with them.

Some of the foot soldiers advanced to the front of the building and, leaning their lances against the walls, began to pile baskets and other debris against the walls, complaining that they had made the long trek for nothing. Others moved about straightening ladders and, muttering similar complaints, began climbing to the second story.

Suddenly, with no hint of warning, Indians silently arose along all levels of the pueblo and unleashed a deadly hail of arrows at point blank range into the soldiers! The attack materialized so quietly it was a minute before the Spaniards realized they were under fire! By then it was too late. Men screamed as arrows pierced unprotected necks, arms and legs. Ladders were overturned, spilling soldiers to the ground where they were easy targets for the warriors above.

More than half the command went down in the first storm of arrows and pandemonium erupted among the rest as they tried to escape the rain of death by fleeing, only to meet a storm of arrows from other warriors who raced around the wings of the pueblo to encircle them. The rout was complete as Indians leapt from the building and attacked the trapped soldiers with hatchets and clubs. The courtyard was filled with dust, war cries, and the shrieks of dying conquistadors.

The mounted officers swung their deadly swords with great effect against the warriors but were overcome by a designated team of Aztecs and Indians focused on getting them off the horses. Seven were quickly disabled by arrows or spears and dragged from the animals. Only Marquez survived, spurring his horse toward the line of fighters between him and freedom. He had no stomach for real combat and thought only to save himself. Somehow he made it through the swirling bodies and choking dust to the outer edge of the battle. One man stood between him and the open desert.

CHAPTER 32

Struggle

In the instant before his horse hit the man, Marquez had a fleeting impression of a headband with two bright feathers sticking out of it in a "V," and something hanging from his right hand. He held no bow or spear and the conquistador experienced a flash of triumph as he swung his sword with all his strength and struck the man perfectly on the rib cage under the left arm as he jumped to avoid the lunging horse. The sword was knocked out of his hand by the impact but as he cleared the battle line, the lieutenant reveled in the thought that cutting a man in half was a satisfying way to make his escape. He could see the cactus landscape ahead and raised his right arm to slap the horse's rump for more speed.

The shock of the blow to his elbow would have pitched him out of the saddle if he hadn't grabbed it in a death grip with his left hand. His right arm was stretched out behind him and felt like it was going to be pulled out of the socket. He stared in horror at the leather cords connected to a heavy pouch that had somehow become wrapped around the elbow. Unable to bend his arm, he looked back and saw the ends of the cords gripped in two hands by the man he thought he had nearly cut in two with the sword! Dragged by the horse, the man was scrambling to get his feet under him and run with the animal. Savagely driving spurs into the sides of the horse, Marquez determined to keep going until he could free himself from the cords, but the straps only tightened on his arm as the increased speed caused the full weight of the man behind to bear on them.

When Cuto had raced out from behind the arms of the pueblo with the Indian warriors the battle had filled the air with choking dust. Arrows fired at point blank range cut down foot soldiers, desperate to escape, causing the survivors to turn back toward the court-yard in complete panic, stirring up even more of the fine white powder.

The Aztec was determined to let no horse go free and when the rider suddenly emerged from the swirling clouds there wasn't time to fire his sling so he held his ground until the last possible second, hoping for an arrow to bring the man down. Jumping sideways to avoid being trampled, Cuto took the sword blow beneath his left arm while simultaneously flinging the loaded sling underhand at the arm holding the blade. The weighted pouch wrapped around the man's elbow three times, tangling itself in such a way that it held fast when Cuto was yanked off his feet, still holding the cords, as the horse sped away.

Only three feet of sling separated Cuto from Marquez's arm, so he was nearly upright as the animal dragged him, and he tried hard to regain his feet but the initial pace was too great as the rider forced his mount ahead. They went on this way for 150 yards: the lieutenant afraid to let go of the saddle with his left hand and unable to pull his right arm forward against the dead weight of the man dragging behind; the Aztec grimly hanging on to the braided leather straps and unsuccessfully trying to get his feet under him.

Finally the horse, lathered with sweat and blowing hard, began to slow despite the spurring. Cuto got purchase with his right foot and then the left; three strides brought him level with the rider and, launching himself into the air, he dragged the conquistador from the animal's back. They tumbled over and over on the ground, still connected by the sling. The Spaniard wound up curled on his side in a fetal position, both hands stretched out toward the Aztec, babbling for mercy. Cuto rose and untangled the sling from the soldier's arm. For a moment he stood, considering whether to brain the man with the still loaded pouch, the memory of the awful night in the storeroom still fresh in his mind.

The sound of drumming hooves in the distance broke the spell. Retrieving the animal was crucial; the coward wasn't worth his attention. Spitting on the groveling figure in disgust, he started trotting after the horse. It was a decision he would later regret.

CHAPTER 33

Swords

Juan couldn't help himself. "He should have split the man's skull with the loaded sling and then gone after the horse!"

"Cowardice is pathetic when it's revealed," the old man replied. "It takes brutality to kill a groveling, defenseless man. Our ancestors have never been known for brutality."

The twins groaned as Great Grandfather finished his coffee and pushed back from the table. It was his way of telling them that the story was over for that morning. They knew better than to ask what was going to happen next, because the answer was always the same: "Guess you'll have to wait until next Saturday."

The pronouncement was invariably accompanied by a sympathetic smile and a twinkle in the old man's eyes.

Juan decided to try to lure him back into the narrative. "What about those swords? Were they any good?"

The old man paused, and then leaned forward to emphasize his point. "Not only good, they were exceptional. For centuries the city of Toledo in Spain has been renowned for its fine steel weapons, these swords would almost certainly have been made there. Horsemen, such as Marquez, would have been issued one about three feet long with a relatively narrow blade, razor sharp on both sides. It would have been flexible enough to bend in a half circle and strong enough to survive a full force blow on a metal helmet. In the hands of a skilled swordsman, it was a devastating weapon. Makes you appreciate the quality of the Incan armor."

Juan whistled softly. "So Marquez's cut at Cuto might really have almost severed his torso, without the shirt?"

"Absolutely. It would have been a killing blow."

"What did the Incan and Aztec people do with captured weapons?"

"Used them I suppose! After they were conquered, however, it was normally illegal for them to possess such weapons. Lets wrap it up; I have to go to Monte Vista."

Juan persisted. "But Great Grandfather, next Saturday we'll be in the mountains with Dad and Mom."

In February, the school in Center always had a four day break over President's Day weekend. The twins looked forward to it every year because it was the one time during the winter when no athletic events were scheduled and the family headed for the mountains to snowmobile. Riding behind their parents on the two powerful Arctic Cat machines was a thrill they had enjoyed ever since they were little.

This year would be different, however, because Dad had surprised them at Christmas with gift certificates good for a two-day rental of a snowmobile from a shop in nearby Monte Vista. For the first time they would have their own machines to ride!

"Bummer." Great Grandfather sounded just like one of their friends. "I don't suppose you two would be willing to give up snowmobiling for more of the story?"

The kids laughed. "There's always another Saturday, but there's only one President's Day weekend. Why don't you drive up and see us off?"

"I might just do that! Tell you what, if you can drag yourselves out of your warm beds tomorrow and be here at 6:00 AM, we can share some huevos rancheros I've got in the freezer and go on with the story before I drive over to Alamosa."

"Deal!" The twins grinned with enthusiasm.

After they washed the dishes, the kids each grabbed a peanut butter cookie and headed for the door.

"I still think he should have brained him!" growled Juan as they headed up the street for home.

CHAPTER 34

Refuge

When Cuto returned to the carnage at the pueblo, leading the horse, some of the warriors wanted to go after Marquez but Feather stopped them.

"It doesn't matter whether he escapes or the expedition fails to return; in either case, the soldiers will mount an attack against us. We've accomplished the objective of capturing horses and now we must hide them and ourselves." He smiled at Cuto. "Thanks to your strategy, we have taken the first step toward balancing power with the conquistadors!"

The Indian casualties were surprisingly light, a testimony to the total surprise of the attack. One man had been killed and four had serious wounds but other injuries were light. A runner was sent to recall those hidden in the hills and within hours, skilled healers were attending to the wounded. The rest of the population prepared to evacuate the pueblo and move to the ancient cliff dwelling.

"If the soldiers know about the canyon, I doubt they have actually found the path off the rim and discovered the cliff house; even so, it would be nearly impossible for them to mount a successful assault against it." Feather announced. "I actually think they will assume we have gone to the mountains in the south rather than the open desert to the east."

"What about the horses?" Cuto wanted to know.

"Five miles below the cliff houses, and on the far side of the canyon, is a hidden valley surrounded by high cliffs. The entrance to it is extremely narrow and almost impossible to find if one doesn't know where it is. Inside is plenty of grass and water for the horses. I discovered it years ago, when hunting in the big canyon, and have always thought it would be a perfect place to defend if the cliff dwelling was compromised. You, your men, and the animals will be safe there."

It was dark when they set out for the canyon with horses, donkeys, and even dogs loaded with food and supplies beyond what the people carried. The dead soldiers had been stripped of weapons and the bodies buried in a ravine a half mile away. The area around the building was carefully swept free of tracks and the whole village traveled single file for the first 10 miles, with three men at the rear using branches to sweep away all traces of their passing.

Walking all night, with only a brief rest at dawn, they reached the rim of the canyon late the following evening. At dawn the Indians began to lower supplies on long ropes down the cliffs while the Aztecs experimented with riding the horses. Ria turned out to be a natural, quickly adapting to the movement of the animal. The others took some tumbles before getting the feel of it, but within a couple of hours all were proficient enough to set out. Feather had described a game trail leading to the canyon floor 11 miles down the rim, after which they would have to backtrack 6 miles to the hidden entrance.

Bidding goodbye to their friends they started off, Ria at the front leading the extra horse packed with supplies. Cuto brought up the rear, herding the loaded donkeys ahead of him. As he watched his wife's body moving in harmony with her horse, black hair swirling gently below the red headband in a soft breeze, Cuto marveled at the benefit of the animals. Not only was he traveling effortlessly, without having to watch where he placed his feet, but also his head was high above the ground, giving him a clear view of the surroundings.

"Horses are going to change the lives of our peoples forever," he thought to himself.

The game trail off the rim was steep and everyone held tight to the horses' manes and leaned back as the animals braced themselves on the descent with rear legs. After they all reached the bottom safely, Mazatl looked back up at the rim far above.

"I'm glad that's over, I've never squeezed anything so tight with my legs as I did this horse on the way down! I thought I was going to be sitting up between its ears!" No one laughed.

It was late afternoon as they started up the canyon in the direction of the cliff house. Just at dusk they crossed a small stream flowing from the eastern cliffs to join the main creek they were following. It was the sign Feather had described and Cuto immediately stopped the group. To the left, 300 yards away, were what seemed to be solid cliffs from which the stream emerged. When they had ridden to within 30 yards, however, he saw that there was a crack in the face of the cliff extending all the way to the rim, 200 feet above. The crack had occurred in such a way that it created a passageway to the left behind the outer face of the cliff, a passage that was almost invisible from a distance because it didn't look like there was any separation in the rock wall. The stream flowed along one side of the 25-foot wide passage, flanked by a sandy floor.

The Aztec slid off his horse and led it into the opening, followed by the others. Steep walls rose on either side, shutting out everything but a sliver of the darkening sky above. The footing was firm and the corridor angled with turns and twists back into the cliff for 60 yards before opening into a beautiful valley surrounded by towering cliffs. Covered in tall grass, it was a half mile long and a quarter mile wide, with groves of cottonwoods marking the path of the meandering stream down the middle. A covey of quail flew up as they emerged from the crack and a herd of grazing deer raised heads at the disturbance. Refracted light from the sunset tinged the top of the cliffs with faint red.

They all stopped in their tracks to stare, speechless in awe.

"It's beautiful," murmured Ria. "Everything is exactly as Feather described; it's a perfect hideout for us and the horses!"

CHAPTER 35

Cave

THE NEXT MORNING work began on their new home and within a month, three small adobe houses were finished and green sprouts were beginning to push up in vegetable gardens near the stream. A rough gate of poles prevented horses from leaving the valley, and a jumble of rock at the hidden entrance had been cleverly fashioned into a disguised lookout station. Runners from Feather had twice assured them that no conquistador patrols had been seen but Cuto remained uneasy and took turns with the others manning the lookout 24 hours a day. He had no doubt that the lieutenant burned for revenge and would make every attempt to find them.

One morning, he set out to explore the upper end of the canyon. On the way he approached the horses, grazing peacefully beside the stream. When he drew close, they raised their heads to stare at him, ears alertly pointed forward. Startled, he stopped dead in his tracks.

"They seem bigger than when we arrived and their coats shine!" He thought, staring in bewilderment.

Preoccupied with building the dwellings and gardens, the Aztecs had paid little attention to the animals for the past month, other than to note that they never seemed to stop grazing. Seeing them now, Cuto began to comprehend that the Aztec's lack of experience with horses had blinded them to the fact that animals they brought to the valley were thin and rundown, possibly to the point of starvation. Unlimited grass and water had worked wonders; they looked and acted like eight completely different animals, snorting and prancing away as he walked toward them. Ria and the others were going to be amazed at the transformation.

Moving on, he came to the cliffs at the upper end of the valley where the creek emerged from a small crevice. A dark spot in brush at the base of the cliff beside the stream caught his eye and, pushing branches aside, he saw the opening to a cave. It was eight feet across and four feet high, the sand around it undisturbed. Kneeling down, he peered in and observed what appeared to be a substantial cavern.

With his curiosity aroused, the Aztec searched among the nearby trees until he found a dead branch with a thick, knotty end. Making a small fire, he ignited the torch and squatted at the entrance, thrusting the flaming branch into the darkness. The light revealed a large chamber extending back into the cliff. It was at least 30 feet wide, with a sandy floor and rock walls fading to blackness beyond the flickering light. The ceiling was 10 feet high. Stooping to enter, he raised the torch as he stood up and was startled by a cloud of bats disturbed by the light; they flitted around the wavering beams for a few minutes before retreating back to the unseen reaches of the cave.

Cuto felt a definite presence to the cavern, it didn't have the feeling of an animal's lair, and he swung his torch around to illuminate the nearby walls. Almost immediately he saw blackened rock to one side of the entrance and his inquiring finger came away dark with soot, many cooking fires had been burned here.

Moving slowly away from the sunlit opening Cuto advanced into the dark, vaguely uneasy about what he might find. Although the medallion was cool, he remembered his grandfather's story about the jaguar attack and he was reaching for the sling when a figure appeared to his left! There was no time for the sling and the Aztec snatched the knife from his belt, whirling to face the attack. Heart pounding, he crouched and thrust the flaming branch forward with his left hand, right hand poised to drive the blade home into his assailant.

CHAPTER 36

Chimney

IN THE SPACE OF A heartbeat Cuto saw that the figure was not made of flesh and blood but was the white outline of a nearly full sized man painted on the rock wall! The round head, with circles for eyes and a straight line for a mouth, and the outlined arms and legs had appeared so lifelike for an instant in the flickering torchlight that he had thought himself under attack! A small chuckle escaped his lips but his heart was still pounding!

Moving closer, he was startled to see the entire wall covered with paintings. They were all sizes and shapes, some recognizable and others not. In addition to the man figure, there were human handprints, large and small, along with drawings of birds, snakes, and insects. Desert sheep were posed in flight, hunters after them with bows and arrows. Among the animal drawings were other human figures, some with odd heads and eyes. He recognized the painting of a jaguar but there was another animal with a blocky body and sharp teeth that he didn't know.

Some of the work was done in tans, reds, and greens, while the rest was simply white like the figure that had seemed to jump at him. It was a fantastic scene! He imagined hands drawing the figures with only the illumination from torches like his own and wondered whether they had belonged to the Ancient Ones of the cliff dwelling.

As he moved along the wall studying the pictures, the torch began to flicker and sputter from a small but distinct current of air. Peering ahead, Cuto saw that he had nearly reached the back of the cavern and, just as the flame went out, observed a dark hole where the side and back walls came together. In pitch-black darkness he turned and saw that he had moved deep into the cave; the mouth was just a small patch of light 150 feet away. Touching the fingers of his right hand to the wall as a guide, he began to make his way back, puzzling over the source of the faint breeze.

Emerging into the sunlight, he realized that the cave mouth was slightly elevated and offered an excellent view down the entire canyon. Anyone approaching could be seen from inside without revealing one's position, although the chamber itself would become a trap if there was an extended siege. He wondered what it had been used for in the past.

Armed with an extra torch, Cuto returned to the cave and proceeded directly to the rear. He found the dark hole was the opening to a narrow fissure extending at a sharp angle away from the main room. From it came a small breath of air that made the torch flicker and he saw it was just high and wide enough to walk through. He heard the sound of running water and realized it led to the underground stream flowing into the valley.

Sure enough, after 30, feet he came to water rushing and bubbling on its way to the outside. Here, a definite draft pushed the flame of the branch downward. Glancing up, Cuto was amazed to see a sliver of daylight far above. There was a cleft in the rock that extended all the way to the surface of the desert floor! As he stared at that tiny patch of blue, something clicked in Cuto's brain. He held the torch over the stream and studied the solid rock wall facing him. Minutes went by and then a broad smile split his face. Cut into the rock was a hole! Squatting, he found another hole below and two more above. The Ancient Ones had been here after all!

Within minutes the Aztec figured out the starting handholds and began his ascent. As with the routes at the cliff house he found the holes deep enough and so regularly spaced that he was able to abandon the torch and climb smoothly in the dark. In 20 minutes he emerged into a pile of rocks set innocuously on the desert floor a few yards away from the rim overlooking his valley. Scattered about were other piles of rock and he realized that the fissure exit had been cleverly designed to match them. Unless one was actually standing on the pile, the opening in the ground could not be seen.

A 20-minute walk brought him to the rim above the houses. Ria and four of the men were working the gardens 200 feet below; he knew that Xpil was on guard in the main canyon. In fact, a few minutes later he was staring down at his friend concealed in the rocks outside the corridor leading to the hidden valley. Where Cuto was standing, the passage was no more than 20 feet wide and an idea began to take root from stories Adzul had told him about his flight from Pattiti 60 years earlier. The Aztecs had work to do along the rim of the corridor.

The twins groaned as the storyteller stood up, indicating that he had run out of time. It seemed like only a minute had passed since he began but they were startled to see the clock registering that it had been an hour and a half!

"We'll clean up, so you can get on the road," Juan said. "You rock for giving us the extra session!"

"My pleasure, I love it as much as you do, and good luck next weekend," replied the old man as he shrugged into his coat and headed for the garage.

CHAPTER 37

Wolf Creek Pass

GREAT GRANDFATHER stepped out of the pickup and pulled on the heavy winter parka with its fur-lined hood. It was the following Saturday morning and bitterly cold at the snowmobile turnout high on Wolf Creek Pass, although the blue sky above promised a beautiful day. Pulling on insulated gloves, he walked back to the trailer attached to his vehicle to help his grandson unload the gleaming Arctic Cat snowmobiles from the rental shop.

"Glad you didn't decide to go to Santa Fe," the younger man exclaimed, "I forgot that we needed an extra trailer for the rental machines."

"I was actually thinking about going before you called; with the kids occupied for the weekend it would have been a good time to visit some old friends down there."

With Juan and Sophia helping, all four machines were unloaded and the extra trailer parked beside the family rig.

"No sense in pulling it all the way to the valley, I'll hook it up when I come back for you this afternoon," said the old man as he watched the family load packs with thermoses of hot soup and sandwiches.

"Are your beepers turned on and set to transmit?" Dad asked.

Both Juan and Sophia pulled the small black devices, attached to cords around their necks, from under their one-piece snowmobile suits and checked to see that the green light was glowing on 'Send.'

"Yes," they answered, tucking the beepers back in.

"Mom?" Their father was a stickler for safety in the backcountry, particularly in the winter, and the family was well trained in the use of the so-called 'beepers.'

The transmitters were part of their safety equipment. When turned on, the devices sent out a continuous signal until turned off at the end of the day. Should anyone become separated from the group, the others would turn their transmitters to 'Receive' and the little machines would begin to pick up the signal of the sending transmitter, indicating the source by a blinking light and a beep. As the devices got closer, the beeps and lights would become more rapid, finally becoming solid in close proximity. Other safety items included collapsible shovels, emergency blankets, and a first aid kit.

"Yes, my beeper is turned on." Mother replied.

After double-checking his own transmitter, Dad climbed on his Arctic Cat and started it, motioning for the others to do the same. They all wore insulated boots, suits, and thick mittens with cuffs reaching well up their forearms. Fleece balaclavas (which pulled completely down over the head and face, leaving only space for the eyes), black helmets and ski goggles completed the attire. Every bit of clothing would be needed against the cold.

They were the first to arrive at the turnout and heavy snow the past two days had wiped out all tracks leading into the forest; at least a foot of white covered every branch on the tall evergreen trees. Wolf Creek Pass always gets heavy snowfall and this year was no exception: 200 inches of snow had already been reported and the biggest storms were still to come in March and April. Excitement filled Juan and Sophia as Dad eased his Arctic Cat over the drift at the edge of the parking lot and headed into the forest.

"See you at 4:30," bellowed Great Grandfather, waving, but his voice was lost in the roar of the machines.

CHAPTER 38

Enthusiasm

WHEN THE FAMILY ARRIVED back at the parking lot, Great Grandfather had already hitched up the spare trailer and was waiting patiently in his warm pickup.

"How'd it go?" he asked when the engines had been shut down.

"Sweet!" exclaimed Sophia as Juan pumped his fist. "We had first tracks all morning until almost 11:00! Dad really knows where to go!"

"Any problem driving yourselves?"

"No way!" Juan's eyes sparkled as he lifted his goggles up on his helmet. "All the lessons with Mom and Dad really paid off!"

On the way home they stopped in South Fork for cookies and hot chocolate. The kids regaled Great Grandfather with stories about carving turns on hillsides and bursting through drifts. Surprisingly, neither had gotten stuck or dumped a machine in the deep snow, a testament to years of riding with their parents and being taught proper technique.

"Same turnout tomorrow?" the old man questioned his grandson.

"No. I want to go a little higher on the pass, the top parking lot, and take the kids to a remote valley not many people know about. The holiday traffic was getting pretty heavy back there this afternoon and it'll be worse tomorrow."

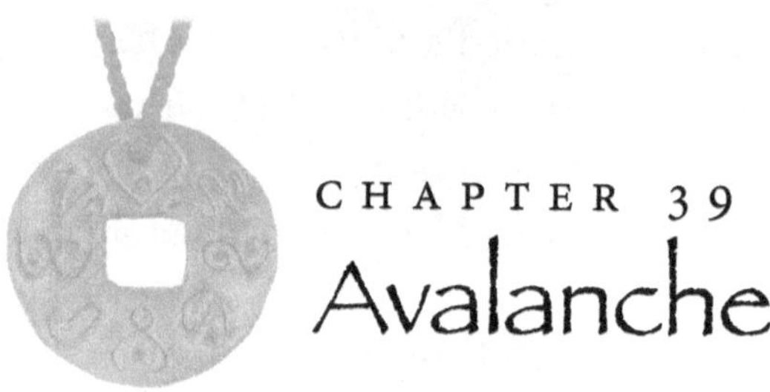

CHAPTER 39

Avalanche

IT STORMED ON THE PASS that night and the next morning Dad headed out from the upper parking lot through 10 inches of new snow. Sophia followed close behind, trailed by Juan, with Mom bringing up the rear. Breaking clouds promised another sunny day and the twins were exhilarated with the prospect of blasting through new powder again. For a while they all made tracks on a lightly forested hillside not far from the turnout, banking and turning in the unbroken white, sending up great sprays of snow to either side. Gradually more and more snowmobiles showed up, creating tracks everywhere, and finally Dad led the way into the vast sweep of mountains in search of more powder. Thirty minutes later they entered a long valley with scattered trees reaching halfway up the slopes to either side. Dad stopped and turned off his engine.

"See the cornice up there?" He pointed to a huge overhanging drift of snow almost a quarter mile above them on the right slope. "When it breaks off, it runs down the hillside on that path through the trees."

Sure enough, they could see a swath through the trees ahead on the right. It was 300 yards wide and reached from the cornice all the way down the steep mountainside to the valley floor.

"Do not go anywhere near the bottom of the valley, it's too dangerous. The left hillside is much flatter; we can play around on it safely."

With that, he started his engine, headed up the gentle slope to their left and began making big turns through the powder. In minutes they were all cutting circles and figure 8s in the snow, engines howling. A bit further up the valley Juan saw a wonderful spot with no trees and headed for it, turning sharply uphill to his left before beginning a big looping turn downhill, throwing a big spray of snow, throttle wide open. It was one of his best maneuvers in two days and he was grinning under the balaclava when the machine hit a buried stump and flipped high in the air, pitching him off like a bronc rider thrown from a horse in the rodeo! He landed 30 feet from where the snowmobile had nosedived into the powder, mad because he was the first to get a machine stuck. As he started to struggle through waist deep snow toward the partially buried Arctic Cat, he realized he would need help.

"Dad will have to tow it out," he said to himself.

Suddenly there was a thunderous 'Boom' from across the valley and he looked up. Where the cornice had been was a huge cloud of white billowing to the sky; as he watched in fascination, it became a massive wave flowing down the hill, rapidly picking up speed and accompanied by a terrifying roar. For an instant he enjoyed the spectacle until, to his horror, he saw that he had crashed his machine along the left hillside at a point directly in line with the slide path. He had followed Dad's instructions and was surely high enough that the avalanche couldn't reach him, but the white cloud was descending incredibly fast and swirling hundreds of feet in the air!

An engine revving to high pitch caught his attention and he turned to see Sophia tearing across the slope toward him. He frantically waved at her to turn back but it was too late; she reached him in seconds and stopped, holding out her left hand. He grabbed it and tried to pull himself free but the snow was too deep. Glancing up, he realized the monstrous avalanche was not going to stop at the valley floor but continue up their side.

"Save yourself!" He screamed, but his words were lost in the deafening chaos of the onrushing avalanche.

Still holding him, Sophia twisted the throttle with her other hand and the snowmobile leapt forward. Juan was jerked free just as the blast of air at the front of the avalanche hit them. The ski-do was blown into the air uphill, spinning like a top in the hurricane-force wind. Sophia was swept off and tumbled through the tumult of wind and snow, somehow managing to cling to her brother in a death-grip. An instant later they were totally encased in a rigid cast of snow and all went quiet.

CHAPTER 40
Search

Juan was choking to death from the snow filling his mouth. With the last breath he possessed, he managed to force the white stuff out and suck in great gasps of air, clenching his teeth to keep the snow out.

His goggles were still on but it was totally dark and he couldn't move a muscle; his body felt like it was entombed in concrete. His left arm was across his waist and the right arm stretched above his head, gloved hand still gripping his sister. He remembered Sophia using her snowmobile to pull him free just before the unbelievable blast of air hit them from the leading edge of the avalanche.

"Mom and Dad will be searching for us with the transmitters," he thought. "It won't be long before they'll start digging. Don't panic, there's nothing you can do anyhow."

What he didn't know was that the avalanche had fanned out as it ran up the opposite side of the valley and measured at least 500 yards across by 300 yards long when it stopped. The twins had been blown at least 80 yards uphill from where they had last been seen. Rescuers would have to move over the whole area foot by foot until they intercepted signals from the transmitters; by then it might be too late.

Suddenly there was heat on his chest, getting more intense by the second. The medallion! Juan thought back to Great Grandfather's stories and hope surged; perhaps it would help them somehow! At first the heat felt good but, as the insulating quality of the suit came into play, it soon became uncomfortable. He started to sweat and worried that he would be in serious trouble with hypothermia if he got cold. He wished the heat would stop but he was utterly helpless to do anything. Hotter and hotter it grew until he began to wonder why he wasn't feeling pain from what must be a terrible burn on his skin. Suddenly a smell rose from the inside of the suit and filled the air space just in front of his mouth. It made him want to retch. It was the smell of burning fabric; the medallion was burning his suit!

On top of the avalanche field, Dad looked at Mom with despair.

"It's too big, we need help."

"I know."

He had seen Juan fall off the snowmobile and was about to head over to help when the cornice broke. Assessing the speed of the rushing snow, he knew that he would never get to his son in time. To his horror, Sophia had gunned her machine forward in an attempt to rescue her brother. He had screamed at her but the roar of the avalanche drowned out the words and he had been forced to watch the two of them catapulted into the air by the gale force wind just before the wall of white struck. In his wildest imagination he had not dreamed an avalanche could run that far up the opposing slope!

"Set your device to 'Receive' and begin to walk across the avalanche field from the top down. The next trip should be no more than three feet below the first; in this way you'll establish a grid. I'm going to the parking area, there's an emergency phone and we can get a rescue crew helicopter in from Alamosa. I'll collect everyone I can to help and be back in less than an hour."

His wife knew that he was right. He was a highly experienced driver and would run the Arctic Cat at full speed the whole way, bringing back other snowmobilers to help. They would need a lot of people quickly if the kids were going to be found alive. She flipped the switch on her beeper, grabbed a shovel, and began to climb to the highest point of the slide field.

CHAPTER 41

Heat

SOPHIA WOKE UP to the sound of her own gasping. By some miracle there was a small, clear space in front of her face so she could breathe but she was locked in a vise of snow, both arms extending over her head. With no frame of reference, she didn't realize that she was completely upside down, feet only 24 inches beneath the surface. Her first thought was for Juan. She remembered holding onto his hand with all her strength as they were literally blown into the air, but everything after that was lost in a blur of roaring and darkness. Had he survived? If so, would they both die before Mom and Dad could find them?

Underneath her, Juan distinctly felt a drop of water hit bare skin where his long underwear should have been. Then another. The heat of the medallion must have burned through his clothes and was melting snow around his chest! In another minute there was a decrease on the pressure against his left arm and then he could move fingers. In another moment the hand and wrist were free and he had a limited range of motion. Suddenly the scene of Adzul tied up at the waterfall flashed into his mind and he knew exactly what to do. Stretching his fingers through the hole burned in his clothes, he grasped the medallion and pulled it out into the cavity that had been created around his chest by the heat. Almost immediately he could feel pressure ease on his upper body, it was like having a flamethrower in his hand!

The silver was throwing off so much heat that he didn't have to actually touch the snow to melt it and in a few minutes he was able to clear a little cave around his helmet. Once he had melted enough snow to slip the helmet off, it was an easy matter to slip the strap off his neck and extend the reach of the hot silver. Within five minutes Juan had freed his lower body and was kneeling in a sort of hole, right arm still extending up to Sophia's hand. He set to work on the trapped arm and quickly melted his way to her glove and gave it a squeeze.

CHAPTER 42
Freedom

Locked in her icy prison, Sophia had no concept of how much time had passed since the avalanche hit. She did remember, however, that victims had to be rescued rather quickly if they were to survive and, even as cold began to creep through the insulation of her suit, she decided she would never give up hope that Dad and Mom would find her in time. To stay positive, she forced herself to think of the things she loved at home.

There was the family dog, Diego, who would get so excited chasing his tail that he lost his balance and fell in a heap! She thought of Mom's incredible tacos, always waiting no matter how late she got home from volleyball practice. She grinned at the memory of beating Juan last summer by landing a 23-inch brown in their competition to lure the biggest trout out of the Rio Grande River. She imagined Great Grandfather's fabulous cookies and thought about his stories of the medallion; how the old man always left them in suspense on Saturday mornings when he ended the story.

Suddenly a shock went through her as she realized her left hand had moved! Not moved, really, but had been squeezed. Then she clearly felt heat through the glove and a moment later her hand was being wiggled! Now she could move her wrist a bit and the heat was at her elbow.

It took 20 minutes for Juan to burn a cave in the snow around Sophia and extricate her from her upside down position. Finally the two were squatting side by side in a cavity bathed by the red glow from the medallion.

"It's just like what happened to Adzul at the river!" Juan marveled, holding the silver in his bare hand. "It's so incredibly hot that it melts the snow instantly but it doesn't burn my skin! It burned through my clothes in no time flat!"

"I was thinking about the stories when I felt my hand move," exclaimed Sophia. "In fact I was so engrossed in remembering how Great Grandfather always ends them in an exciting part that I thought I had imagined your squeeze. I can't believe we were still holding hands; we should have been torn apart when the wind hit! I bet Mom and Dad are worried sick."

"Yep, let me see what I can do to get us out of here."

No sooner had he begun melting the snow over their heads than it began to grow lighter and a minute later they poked heads and shoulders out of the avalanche field. Above them, a hundred yards away, they could see the figure of their mother trudging along staring down at the transmitter held in one hand, a survival snow shovel gripped in the other.

"Mom!" they shouted in unison.

CHAPTER 43

Perspective

"**I** STILL CAN'T believe it! The medallion saved us just like it saved Adzul when it burned through his ropes at the waterfall 500 years ago!" Juan was still staggered by the thought.

"There's also the matter of us staying together in that awful air blast," Sophia added. "I don't believe anyone is strong enough to hold on through that! But there we were, glove to glove under the snow."

Great Grandfather nodded, eyes lost in thought. "There's something about the medallion protecting our family that we'll never understand. It's been going on since the very beginning, 500 years ago."

It was a week after the avalanche and the twins had arrived at his house for breakfast and more of the story about Cuto. The events of the previous weekend were still fresh in their minds, however, and conversation at the table had centered on the engraved piece of silver.

"Did it ever get hot with you?" Sophia wanted to know.

"Once, but in a different context," the old man replied somewhat mysteriously. "Did you replace the snow mobile suit?" He asked Juan, changing the subject.

"Yeah, the old one was trashed. There must have been an 18-inch hole in the chest! Mom found one in Alamosa that has cool electric green accents! I'm fired up to wear it!"

"Oh, are you going again?"

"Yup, Dad says it's like getting back on a horse after you fall off, so he rented machines for two weeks from now."

"How do you feel about it?" Great Grandfather fixed his eyes on Sophia.

"Great! It was a scary time but the Arctic Cats are still fun. Dad admitted the mistake was his; he shouldn't have taken us into the valley with such a huge cornice, although the men who came back with him said they had never seen evidence of a slide running anywhere near so high up that opposite hill."

True to his word, Dad had made a high-speed run to the parking area and called the Forest Service; within minutes a mountain rescue helicopter was on its way from Alamosa. He had arrived back at the avalanche site just after the kids popped through the snow, five other snow machines racing behind him. After the relief of finding the twins safe, the men had stared at the slide path in amazement.

"It's incredible that the kids wound up just under the surface and got out so quickly, that's the biggest avalanche I've ever seen," commented one.

Dad noted the look that passed between his children.

"The wind force must have been nearly 100 MPH at the lead edge," said another in awe.

"That Arctic Cat flew through the air like a plastic toy," Dad had acknowledged, emphasizing the point by nodding at a handle bar sticking out of the snow 200 feet away.

Alerted by a friend at the hospital in Del Norte, Great Grandfather had arrived just as the helicopter carrying the kids and Mom settled on the pad. An examination by one of the docs showed no ill effects and they were soon released. The talk during the rest of that weekend, and the week that followed, had been about the improbability of such a monster avalanche.

"A 500 year event," one of the Forest Service men had called it in a debriefing session.

CHAPTER 44

Character

Now, as he watched the twins devour pancakes and elk sausage smothered in blueberry syrup (in the way that only teenagers can), Great Grandfather fixed his gaze on Sophia.

"So, do you remember our conversation at Christmas?"

She glanced at him with a questioning look; her mouth was full of food and she couldn't speak.

"We talked about courage and determination under extreme circumstances. You said that you could never have gone on like Swallow after she was brutalized."

"That was when you told us about Ernest Shackleton," Juan interjected. "It made such an impression on me I looked him up online."

Sophia nodded, swallowing her mouthful of pancakes.

"Excellent," said the old man, without taking his eyes off the girl. "Wouldn't you agree that the two of you faced an extreme circumstance last Sunday?"

"That's for sure!" The kids replied in unison, with the uncanny knack twins have for knowing what each other is going to say.

"Your actions didn't match up so well with one who said that she never had to face life or death situations and would just give up if she did."

Sophia held out both hands, "Great Grandfather! Juan was trapped, I couldn't let him die could I?"

"Of course not, although you could easily have been killed trying to save him. The point is you didn't hesitate for an instant; you did the courageous thing. Some people might criticize, saying you should have saved yourself and losing one life is better than losing two, but that didn't enter your mind did it?"

"Absolutely not, I was going to yank him out of that snow, no matter what! Anyway, I just did what I had to. Swallow's situation was different."

"Not really," the old man's voice was soft. "She had to keep going in order to survive, just as Shackleton had to keep going to save his men. You kept going to save your brother. You don't know how proud I am of you." He cleared his throat and turned away to the stove for another cup of coffee, brushing a hand across his eyes.

When he turned back, Juan had pulled the medallion from under his wool shirt and was studying it. "Those men thought we were only two feet under the snow but they were wrong. Sophia's boots were two feet down but her head was probably five feet under and my head was at least two feet below her. But for this incredible piece of silver, it would have probably been over before they found us. How is it possible that it keeps working miracles after 500 years?"

"I don't know," replied Great Grandfather. "What I do know is a great trust was bestowed on the family when Qist passed the medallion to Adzul, and that trust has been faithfully kept for five centuries by each family member that wore it. Although the medallion alerted them to danger and sometimes protected them, as it did you last weekend, every heir faithfully discharged his or her obligation without seeing the secret revealed. If the two of you are indeed meant to discover the mystery, our family will have answered its calling with honor."

There was a moment's pause while the twins contemplated this statement. Then Great Grandfather leaned forward with a smile to dispel the seriousness of the moment.

"Now, where was I before all these snowmobile problems occurred?"

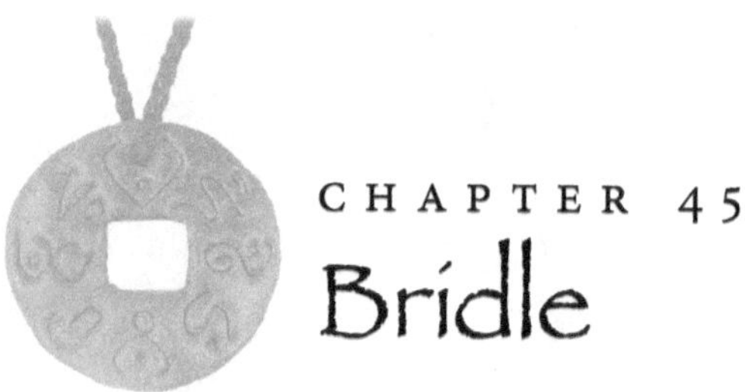

C H A P T E R 4 5

Bridle

When Cuto returned and told Ria about the changes in the horses, she was excited. Working with the horses had never been far from her mind and she had often stared at them grazing in the distance during the construction of the little settlement. The next morning she filled a small sack with dried maize and walked through the deep grass to where the little herd was grazing. When she drew close she was amazed at the difference in the animals. Bodies and necks had filled out, even the faces looked fuller! Long tails swished flies off backs that glistened in the sun and every head was raised, ears forward, at her approach.

Talking softly, Ria stopped 20 feet away and held out a handful of kernels. The jet-black stallion was the first to move, bobbing its head and walking over to nuzzle a mouthful of corn. The gray followed suit and before long all eight were crowded around her for snacks. She stroked their cheeks and necks, delighted to have them so close and to feel the energy and vitality of their bodies. When the maize ran out and the horses returned to the grass Ria wandered among them, running her hands along necks and backs. The animals seemed totally comfortable in her presence and occasionally bumped her with their heads as she tickled their ears.

That afternoon Ria fetched a bridle from among those worn by the horses when they had ridden to the valley. Sitting on a stump in the sun, black hair glistening, she turned the heavy contraption over and over until she grasped how it worked. Her concentration was so focused that she hardly realized her husband had squatted beside her until his hand gently touched her shoulder.

"It's too heavy and I think the metal piece that goes in the mouth is cruel," she said, fingering the pointed part of the bit that rested on the horse's tongue.

"Why don't you make one of your own?" Since childhood Ria had amazed him with her creativity and he loved watching her wrestle with a new problem, forehead slightly furrowed, beautiful eyes lost in thought.

It took numerous trips to the herd for fitting but when she finished, her braided leather creation resembled a modern hackamore and was much lighter than the Spanish bridle. The reins were made of one length of braided leather, tied to the headpiece under the horse's jaw, and looped over its neck so the rider could let go of it to use both hands without dropping loose ends to the ground.

The day came when Ria slipped her headpiece on the black horse and led it to a nearby log. Talking softly and stroking its neck, she used the log to boost herself onto the animal's back, one hand holding the rein and the other gripping a fistful of mane. The horse shook its head once or twice and pranced a few steps, but years of training came back and it soon stood quietly. When Ria leaned forward and pressed with her knees, it began to walk toward the houses.

Cuto and the other men looked up from their work as she approached. The horse's head was up, eyes and ears attentive, robust body in stark contrast to the plodding animals that had carried them to the valley. They watched in silence as she guided the black this way and that around the gardens and houses.

"I can't believe the change in that stallion," said Cuto in awe. "When we learn to ride, we will be a force to be reckoned with! Look at Ria, you would never know this is only her second time." He smiled proudly.

The beautiful girl, her long black hair a shining reflection of the stallion's coat, was moving in harmony with the animal as though she had ridden all her life.

From that day forward Ria rode one or more of the horses every morning. As she grew familiar with them, she learned that each had a personality, just like people. The bay horse, with black mane and tail, enjoyed sleeping on the ground. It could often be found fully stretched out, snoring quietly, while the rest of the herd grazed peacefully around it. The gray and the pinto could be found every afternoon standing side by side, head to rump, each gently swishing flies away from the other's face with its long trail. The yellow horse, that Ria called Sunflower, always nuzzled the woman's hair in search of a stray kernel of maize.

Most of them, like the black, loved to run and only needed a forward lean and the touch of her heels to race ahead. A few were surprisingly agile, able to turn so quickly at a full run that she frequently fell off! As her skills improved, however, she began to stay glued to the animals' backs, no matter what the pace or change in direction.

Gradually the men learned to ride, copying Ria's style of a soft voice and repeated praise to their mounts. All were good students, but Cuto excelled. Like Ria, he had a natural feel for the horse and quickly developed such balance that, at any gait, he moved in complete harmony with the animal. Soon the Aztecs were engaged daily in races and high-speed games and, as time went by, noticed more energy, stamina, and liveliness in the horses.

"I think they're like people," Xpil commented. "The more exercise they have, the stronger they get! The stronger they get, the more they enjoy using their strength!"

CHAPTER 46

Lion

THE BLACK STALLION was the protector of the herd, although there seemed to be no danger in the canyon. Grabbing a mouthful of grass, he would raise his head to chew while looking this way and that. Surrounded by towering red cliffs, the secluded valley seemed safe and secure, but one afternoon Ria saw the entire band suddenly race from one side to the other. Only the stallion remained, ears flat back on lowered head, staring into the grass. Suddenly he charged forward, front hooves striking out. Even from a distance she saw a flash of tawny color in the grass and then the horse was on it, front hoofs stomping again and again. A tortured scream, sounding almost human, echoed off the canyon walls. The horse finally backed away, shaking his head, tail up, and stood for a few minutes before turning away to rejoin the others.

Calling to Cuto, Ria grabbed an atlatl and spear as they set out to the scene of the disturbance. There, in a patch of flattened and bloody grass, they found the mangled body of a mountain lion.

"It must have come down the cliffs somehow," Cuto speculated. "It should have stayed in the desert!"

In observing the horses, however, Ria came to realize that while the stallion provided protection, the real leader was a gray mare. She was the one that made the decision to go for water or find a different place to feed. There seemed to be no signal, but when the mare moved off the rest would follow with the stallion bringing up the rear.

The youngest horse was buckskin, with dark mane and tail, and given to sneaking up on some of the others to nip them on the rump. After this had gone on for a while, the mare would carefully move through the herd, appearing to graze, until quite close to the offending youngster. Then with a sudden squeal she would charge the buckskin, driving him well away from the herd. For the rest of that day, and even into the following day, whenever the buckskin tried to rejoin the herd, the gray was there to drive him off about 100 yards. Finally, with head lowered in submission and eyes averted, he would be allowed to join the others.

Strengthened by the wonderful grass in the valley, the horses were sometimes given to running for the sheer joy of it. One would take off at full speed and the others would follow, heads outstretched and tails streaming behind, thundering hoofbeats echoing off the cliffs. If all seven Aztecs happened to be riding and someone proposed a race, the horses seemed to understand and dashed away with little urging, the riderless eighth animal bringing up the rear!

CHAPTER 47

Discovery

Each week Cuto, Ria, and one of the others would make the five-mile trip up the main canyon to the cliff dwelling. For a time after the battle, Pueblo scouts had seen Spanish patrols in the distance but, as the weeks passed, fewer and fewer were observed and none ventured toward the canyon.

"From a distance the desert seems flat and endless to the east; our canyon is invisible almost until you reach the rim," Feather observed. "The mountain ranges to the south and west are the most logical places to hide and they must think we've taken refuge there. In mountain terrain, they would be vulnerable to ambush so they have probably given up the search."

His theory was correct. Marquez burned to avenge his humiliation at the pueblo but Rodriguez, suspecting the Indians had holed up in the mountains, refused to let his soldiers search there. The forested canyons and ravines were ideal cover for an attack and he couldn't afford more casualties.

Gradually, new recruits arrived in Santa Fe until the garrison was completely replaced. Only Marquez wasn't transferred because the commanding officer in Mexico refused to sign papers returning the insubordinate officer to his ranks. But the lieutenant had become so obsessed with revenge that the extended duty was welcome. Realizing that Colonel Rodriguez and Father Montoya desired to reestablish peace with the Indians, he secretly began to assemble a small group of disgruntled men from the newcomers. Whenever possible he volunteered for patrols, seeking any hint of his hated adversaries' whereabouts.

One day he rode further into the eastern desert than he had before and stumbled onto the canyon. Far below were two Indians on horses with deer carcasses draped across their mounts' withers. Careful to remain unseen, Marquez followed from above until he saw them disappear into the opposing cliffs, behind which he could see another valley.

Cuto's eyes flew open in the dark. The embers in the corner fireplace of the little adobe house had gone out. Ria was breathing softly beside him and across the room Swallow murmured in her sleep; she had come back with them from the cliff dwelling to see the horses. All was quiet, but the medallion was hot on his skin! He placed a hand on his wife's shoulder.

"Something is wrong," he whispered in her ear. "Get Swallow outside and hide in the trees."

He grabbed armor shirt and sling without waiting for an answer and slipped noiselessly from the house. In the faint light of the stars everything seemed normal but the medallion told him otherwise. Racing on silent feet to the small house where the Aztec men slept, he whispered a word of warning before speeding down the narrow passage toward the main canyon. The corridor was in deep darkness as he ran silently along its twists and turns. Stopping 50 feet from the opening, the Aztec studied the jumble of rocks where Coyotl was stationed on guard. Nothing moved in the faint starlight.

Cupping hands to mouth, Cuto made the soft sound of a hooting night owl. There was no reply. Inching forward, he peered out onto the main canyon. There was a cluster of shapes grouped under the cottonwoods by the stream 300 yards away, but the moonless night made it difficult to discern anything clearly. He was about to step into the open when he spotted movement in front of the sentry post!

In the next instant, the indistinct shapes of ten men materialized beside the sentry rocks, one pointing straight at Cuto, invisible in the deep shadows. As the man moved, starlight glinted faintly off a sword blade. A conquistador patrol had found them! As he was silently backing away, a hand lightly touched his shoulder; the other Aztecs had joined him.

"There are soldiers out there," he spoke in an undertone.

"What do you want us to do?" murmured Xpil.

"Take Ria and Swallow up the cave to the rim. You know what to do when we give the signal. The rest of you get your weapons."

"We'll be ready my love. Be careful." He was startled to hear his wife then, with a whisper of feet on the sand, she and Xpil were gone.

"We're already armed," Mazatl breathed.

"Good. Coyotl didn't answer my call; he may be dead. The soldiers seem uncertain about entering the passage in the dark. If they do, we'll ambush them right here. If they wait until dawn, we'll use the plan we designed when I found the chimney."

Ria swung Swallow up behind her on the black horse and, closely followed by Xpil on the pinto, raced up the valley. They flew past the herd, which nickered greetings, and five minutes later reached the cave. It took only minutes to light a small fire and ignite torches from the supply Cuto had gathered. Handing one to Ria, Xpil led the way into the cavern and back to the passageway.

They had practiced many times for this situation. Swallow went first, locating the starting handholds by the light of the two torches. As she disappeared up into the darkness, Ria handed her flaming knob to Xpil and followed, hands and feet slipping smoothly into the ancient cuts. Propping the branches against the wall, the Aztec found the starting holes before the flames sputtered out and began his climb. Shortly thereafter all three emerged on the desert floor above.

Twenty minutes later they were at the rim over the narrow valley entrance. Looking down into the dark at the place where they had left their companions, Xpil cupped his hands and gave the soft hoot of an owl. For a moment it was quiet and then an answering hoot sounded from nearly 200 feet below.

"The soldiers haven't attacked," he said softly. "They're waiting for dawn."

Lieutenant Marquez had indeed decided to wait until dawn to attack, secure in the belief that he had trapped some of the Indians from the pueblo. He wanted to utterly annihilate them in daylight, lest any escape under cover of darkness. So far his strategy had been a complete success. Under the guise of a hunting expedition, he and his handpicked team had left Santa Fe the day before, lightly dressed and carrying hunting lances. Swords and a blunderbuss were concealed in their bedrolls. They arrived at the trail down to the floor of the main canyon just before sunset.

With the utmost care they led their horses for the last half mile before the hidden passage and picketed them along the stream well away from the entrance; he was certain they hadn't been detected. Armed as they were, he was confident of their ability to deal with the Indians in a surprise attack. As he waited for daylight, the conquistador smiled. When he had found the canyon, and later the game trail down into it, his luck had begun to change and now he was going to enjoy taking his full measure of revenge.

"Life on this forsaken outpost isn't so bad after all," he gloated as the faint light of dawn crept down the canyon walls.

CHAPTER 49
Ruse

On the rim above, Xpil, Ria, and Swallow lay on their stomachs peering down into the shadows. As the black gradually gave way to gray, they could make out the shapes of 15 soldiers sitting among the boulders. Glancing across the canyon, Ria's heart beat with excitement as she identified their horses staked out by the stream. If the animals could be captured, it would almost triple the size of their herd!

A pile of rocks and boulders, 5 feet high and 40 feet long, flanked the three observers, inspired by Cuto's memory of Incan defenses against the horse soldiers. He and the men had spent two weeks building three of these mounds along the rim of the entry corridor, one at either end and one in the middle. Each was cleverly balanced on a platform of logs in such a way that the whole mass could easily be dislodged onto the floor below by raising two long poles inserted among the logs from behind.

All at once, movement at the boulders caught Xpil's attention. The soldiers were stirring. Four men started in the direction of the horses and he realized they were planning to execute a mounted attack.

"We can't let them reach the horses!" Ria whispered urgently. There was no time to lose!

The Aztec nodded and hooted like a great horned owl on its last hunt before daylight. The warning wasn't necessary. From his position inside the fissure, Cuto had also seen the four men start for the horses and understood their intent. Whispering rapidly, he reviewed plans with his men. Tenoch and Patli were sent to the other end of the chasm with all the weapons. He and Mazatl, slinging arms around each other's shoulders, burst into loud and raucous singing and staggered like drunken men out into plain sight.

CHAPTER 50

Pursuit

Marquez leaped to his feet, sword in hand. He couldn't believe his good fortune. Coming right toward him were two drunken Indians singing at the top of their lungs! The fools were probably guards left to watch the entrance. No need for the horses now; with these idiots dead he and his men could catch the rest before they woke up and exterminate them. Yelling at the four men to return, he stepped toward the Indians. As he did, a crooked smile twisted his mouth; clearly visible in the growing light were white scars on the thighs and legs of the man to the right, scars from his own whip. He wouldn't kill this one outright but would break both legs and leave him for later sport.

The singers halted and stared at the soldiers with slack-jawed confusion for a moment before throwing their arms in the air and bolting back into the passage with ear splitting shrieks.

"Stop them before they alert the others," roared Marquez leading the way at a run.

The men swarmed behind him, bloodlust in their eyes. Each had acquired a taste for torturing and abusing Indians and their warped minds thirsted for more. With arms flailing, the two Indians seemed to be within easy grasp; however, every time Marquez or one of the men aimed a vicious sword thrust at them, they managed to stay just out of reach. The enraged conquistadors sprinted after them through the twisting passage. A couple of lances were thrown but sharp turns in the cleft caused them to bounce harmlessly off the rock walls.

On the rim above, the three observers raced ahead of the chase. When they arrived at the last pile of boulders, Xpil and Swallow swerved behind it, each grabbing the end of a pole; Ria crouched to one side peering into the chasm, right arm raised overhead.

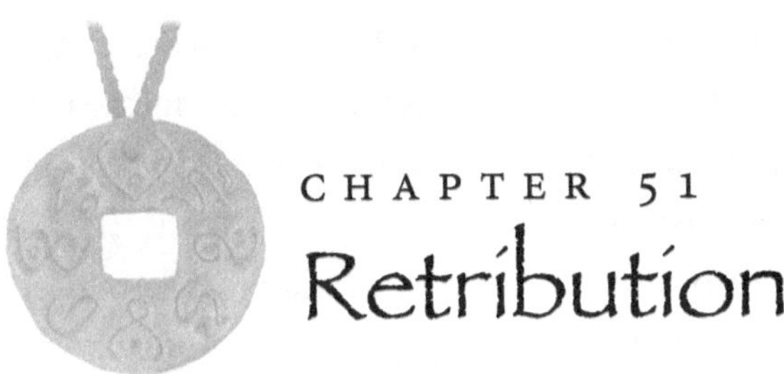

CHAPTER 51
Retribution

As Marquez charged along the passage, the frustration and rage he experienced since his humiliating defeat at the pueblo, combined with his rabid hatred of Indians, caused something to snap in his brain. Forgetting the need for silence, he tipped back his head and gave vent to a bloodcurdling scream. It was like a signal to his half crazed men and wild, inarticulate yells answered, echoing off the rocks with an unearthly sound.

Suddenly the Aztecs sped up and disappeared around a bend. When the pursuers turned the corner they could see daylight no more than 50 yards away; they had reached the entrance to the valley. Screaming and snarling like a pack of hunting wolves, the soldiers ran straight into a hail of spears launched from atlatls with deadly accuracy by four men standing 50 feet away!

With no armor or shields the soldiers were easy targets, packed together as they were in the narrow confines of the corridor. Four went down immediately, pierced through by shafts hurled with tremendous velocity. Almost instantly the atlatls were reloaded and another barrage fired. Four more conquistadors fell as others, rage disintegrating into fear, scrambled to get out of the way of the third volley.

The screams of the wounded mingled with the shouts of men fighting each other to get back around the corner to safety. Marquez had miraculously escaped the first volley of spears by spinning his body sideways at the last moment; the shaft aimed at him had actually torn through his shirt on its way to impaling the man immediately behind. Darting behind two soldiers for protection, he managed to gain the shelter of the corner. Unwilling to face the murderous spears at close range, the surviving seven men surrounded him.

"We out number them! There's only four. Charge you cowards!" Crazed though he was, with animal cunning the lieutenant sought to protect his own skin. But no one moved.

Peeking around the rock, Marquez was shocked to see the spearmen fleeing into the valley.

"They're running away!" He bellowed, grabbing the harquebus from one of the men. "I'll show you, follow me!"

With that, the lieutenant raced out of hiding. Emboldened by the sight of the running Indians, the other men followed, leaping over the bodies of their dead and dying comrades. Reaching the open spot where the Aztecs had made their stand, Marquez paused momentarily to fire the harquebus, his men crowding around. At that instant, Ria dropped her hand.

There was a flash of light, a cloud of white smoke, and a loud 'boom' as the weapon fired. Noting with satisfaction that one of the fleeing men stumbled and fell, the lieutenant threw down the spent weapon and started after them, sword in hand. Somewhere his mind registered that the passage had become dark and he glanced up, wondering at the cause. It was the last thought he ever had.

With a thunderous crash, several tons of rock hit the floor. Dust boiled out into the valley and billowed from the rim above in a great gray cloud…followed by deathly silence.

CHAPTER 52

Aftermath

THE FOUR MEN BELOW cautiously approached the rubble, weapons ready. Nothing moved. Rock completely filled the narrow canyon to a depth of almost three feet; only one hand sticking from the debris gave evidence to what lay underneath. Even the birds and insects had gone quiet, as though overcome with the enormity of what had just transpired.

Cuto looked up to see the figures of Xpil and the two females highlighted in the first rays of the sun. He waved his arm to indicate it was over, and they began to walk back to the chimney.

The others stood silently beside him, shocked by the totality of their victory and suddenly feeling exhausted.

"Without the drunken ruse, they would have had us," observed Patli. "On horseback they would have come too fast for Ria to have timed the rock fall. As it was, they almost ran from under it when we pretended to flee. If they hadn't stopped to fire the blunderbuss, some would have gotten through." He suddenly collapsed, holding his stomach, blood seeping between his fingers.

The others leaped to his side. There was a hole the diameter of an arrow shaft in his left side and a corresponding ragged hole in his back where the piece of shrapnel had exited.

"There was a sound like a swarm of bees when it hit," gasped Patli. "But I had no trouble getting up." His head slumped and he passed out.

They carried him hurriedly to one of the houses and bandaged him front and back before wrapping his midsection with a length of soft cloth.

"I'm not sure how that weapon works but one of Feather's braves told me it rarely hurts anyone," commented Mazatl.

"Apparently the problem is not with the weapon but with the one who uses it," said Cuto dryly. He eyed the blood already beginning to stain the cloth; if his friend died he would never forgive himself for not killing the Spaniard at the pueblo fight.

Asking Tenoch to watch their wounded companion until Ria returned, he and Mazatl set out to learn about Coyotl's fate and recover the horses. They were crossing the rubble when there was a shout from the other side. It was their comrade, staring in awe at the mass of broken rock.

"I had no idea it would work like this," he stated somberly as they reached him.

"They never saw it coming," Cuto said gravely. He felt no exaltation, just relief that his little community had survived.

On the way to get the horses, Coyotl explained what had happened.

"They were so quiet that I didn't see them approach in the dark, but the leader gave them away with one low command just as they got to the rocks. When I heard you hoot, they were all around me and I couldn't answer. All I could do was curl up on the ground behind the boulders and hope they didn't find me. A couple of men were sitting no more than two feet away but they went to sleep waiting for dawn. When you two pulled your stunt, they were so distracted that I could have stood up and they wouldn't have noticed me!

"After they disappeared I moved to a better position for ambushing anyone that came back. The sound of the rock hitting the floor was thunderous, even out there, and I knew you had sprung the trap. When no one appeared, I came to investigate."

"No survivors," said Cuto simply.

By the time the men had managed to lead all 15 horses over the rubble, Xpil and the two women had returned and Ria was attending to Patli's wound. Xpil strode over and put his hand on Coyotl's shoulder.

"I thought we'd lost you."

"I had to go into hiding like a fawn when wolves are near." Coyotl grinned. "But the wolves never smelled me!"

CHAPTER 53
Horsemanship

RIA AND SWALLOW spent a long time making and applying poultices to Patli's wounds. When they were finished, the Aztec was awake and asking in a weak voice about Coyotl. After being reassured that his friend was fine and would visit him later, the wounded man drifted off to sleep again. Cuto, who had been present since returning with the horses, stayed with the patient while Ria and Swallow walked outside to see the 15 new animals.

"Look how thin they are!" Swallow gasped.

Indeed, these horses stood out in stark contrast to their own sleek mounts. Ribs protruded, coats were dull, straggly manes and tails hung limply.

"We could barely drag them away from that good grass by the cottonwoods," Mazatl observed.

"Our horses probably looked just like these when we arrived," said Ria. "We just didn't know the difference."

The contrast was even greater when the new arrivals were stripped of saddles and bridles and turned loose in the valley. Half starved, they immediately began to tear off great mouthfuls of feed, hardly raising heads as the original herd spotted them and came galloping to investigate. The new animals were completely passive as the others pranced among them.

"Our horses look larger somehow." Swallow was amazed.

"It's only because they've filled out, are rested, and in good condition." Ria replied. "Wait and see; the new ones will start to look better in a few weeks."

"I can't wait!" cried the girl but her tone was worried.

The first order of business was to clear out the passageway. The avalanche had been so successful that it completely filled the corridor from one side to the other, damming the stream. It took hours before the water was again flowing through to the main canyon, and it was days before the rest of the rubble was cleared.

Mindful of the need to slow attackers, particularly those on horseback, Cuto used the debris to build abutments six-feet high, and five-feet thick, jutting from either side of the passage underneath the reconstructed boulder pile above. Similar gates were erected below the two other deadly stacks of rock on the rim. There was only enough room for one horse at a time to pass between the ends of the walls, and a cleverly constructed ledge on the backside allowed defenders to launch weapons at an oncoming enemy.

"No one's going to be able to race through the passage and avoid our little surprises from the sky," Cuto announced grimly.

Patli endured several days of intense fever but when it broke he began to recover rapidly. In two weeks he was spending hours sitting against a tree along the stream and two weeks after that he started taking gentle rides.

True to Ria's prediction, by then the 15 new horses had begun to take on a different look. Bodies filled out, coats began to shine, and there was a noticeable change in vitality. Listless and disinterested in anything but grazing when they arrived, now every head came up, ears pricked forward, when anyone approached. Like the others, they were quickly won over by handfuls of maize from Ria and Swallow and followed them around in a cluster whenever the two ventured out with their sacks of corn.

"It's amazing," Cuto remarked to the other men as they watched 23 horses crowd around the women. "Those two have a natural affinity for the animals!"

The new horses were gradually worked into the exercise routine as well, so that all riders began working with at least two animals a day. Four months after establishing their new home, the Aztecs had become proficient horsemen and often visited the cliff house to demonstrate their skills.

During one such trip, Feather watched his daughter ride a gray through a twisting obstacle course at a dead run. With the girl's hands close to its neck the horse did not appear to be guided, but knee pressure and slight shifts of her body communicated precisely where she wanted the animal to go.

"Why doesn't she fall off?" Swallow's mother gasped, hand to her mouth in amazement as the girl executed an abrupt 180-degree change of direction, her body glued to the horse's back.

"Ria has a gift for training us as well the horses," Cuto beamed with pride. "Swallow caught on faster than the men, although she had plenty of falls and bruises along the way!"

"It's time my warriors learned to ride. I need a horse for every man," a determined Feather exclaimed.

"We'll start training immediately. One day you'll have a whole herd of horses, my friend," the Aztec replied.

During the same visit Feather told Cuto that he would be taking the people back to the pueblo in the spring.

"We are all tired of living in the cliffs and want to go home. I've sent scouts into Santa Fe and they report there are new troops and a shortage of fresh food. Some of the distant pueblos have sent traders but it takes time to transport the produce."

"Does your pueblo still stand?"

"Yes. My men report that a fire was started, and part of one wing damaged, but apparently the adobe was too thick. Two or three week's work will restore it." He grinned. "It seems our ancestors passed on excellent construction techniques!"

CHAPTER 54
Bareback

GREAT GRANDFATHER paused for a swallow of coffee. Another week had passed and the twins were seated at his kitchen table, while outside a raging blizzard created a total whiteout. All athletic contests in the area had been cancelled and people warned against the –30 wind chill. Juan and Sophia had simply donned their snow mobile suits, boots, goggles, helmets, and elbow length insulated mittens and trudged the three blocks to their relative's house. No mere blizzard could keep them away from the tale of the medallion!

"It would be like barrel racing," Sophia exclaimed.

"What would?" questioned her brother.

"What they were doing with the horses," she answered. "I picture them at a dead run, weaving around obstacles, like piles of rock, then reversing direction just as the girls do on the third barrel before they head to the finish line. The big difference is these riders were bareback!

"Imagine," she went on, "watching the girls run the barrel race bareback at the Stock Show."

Juan's mind went back to the competition they had seen six weeks before in Denver. The horses came out of an alleyway into the arena at a dead run to execute a clover leaf pattern of spinning turns around three barrels before tearing back to the laser beam finish line. He pictured the riders, hair flying behind the cowboy hats jammed on their heads, holding the saddle horn as the horses spun around each barrel…

"Wait a minute," he exclaimed, "I remember all of them holding the horn during those races!"

"Exactly my point," replied his sister.

"Could it be done without a saddle?" Juan asked, turning to the old man.

"Absolutely. Less than 250 years after Cuto and Ria arrived in Santa Fe the great horse culture of the Indians had spread throughout the west. Horses were so important that stealing them from one another was a prime focus of the Indians. When the whites began to encroach on their hunting grounds, mounted warriors fought them. During the Indian wars of the 1860s and '70s, the professional soldiers of the US Cavalry considered the Plains Indians equal to the finest horse soldiers in the world! That should tell you something about their riding skills!"

"Are you going to tell us about that?" The boy's eyes lit up.

"Not just yet." The brown face wrinkled in a smile. "Suffice it to say, Ria, Swallow, Cuto and the others could indeed have ridden a barrel race at full speed… bareback!" He rubbed his chin, eyes half closed as his memory returned to the past.

CHAPTER 55

Reconciliation

Before long, the spring rains started and flowers again pushed up through the hard soil to paint the desert with color. On a beautiful, cloudless day Cuto rode to the cliff dwelling with Ria and Swallow. It was empty. A crow flew out of a doorway high above on the second story and cried raucously at them.

True to his word, Feather had moved his people back to the pueblo and only itinerant breezes occupied the ancient building. The three sat on their horses watching mud swallows busily constructing little round houses on the upper edge of the huge cave.

"With the horses, we can easily slip in and out of the pueblo at night," said Swallow, hoping to see her parents.

"Yes, but not too soon," replied Cuto. "No doubt the conquistadors are wondering about their lost men and may have lookouts watching your people. Your father will send word when it's safe."

"In the meantime," added Ria, with a knowing look in her eye, "all the horses need as much exercising as we can give them."

Since she had come to love riding more than anything, the girl was smiling happily as they turned to leave.

Cuto was right. As soon as it was known in Santa Fe that the pueblo had been reoccupied, six friars led by Father Montoya paid the Indians a visit. The Indians had always trusted Montoya and food was quickly prepared for him and his men. Sitting on blankets in front of the building, the friar courteously waited until the meal was finished before addressing the chief.

"My friend, we have not seen your people for many months." Fluent in the Pueblo language, the priest spoke quietly.

"Yes. We thought it wise to leave the pueblo after the fight with the soldiers."

"The Commander was surprised that you felt it necessary to break into the storeroom and remove the captive. He would have been freed the next day."

"He was nearly dead from the whipping and three days' dehydration. We thought he would be slain the next day; and for nothing more than looking at the horses!"

The Father was careful to keep his gaze steady but inside he was startled. He had been present when the commanding officer ordered the prisoner held for three days on water rations only. Marquez testified later that he scrupulously followed orders. Montoya had known Feather for a long time and had never heard him lie. Something was amiss.

"I assure you that Colonel Rodriguez had no intention of injuring the man. I was present when he gave the orders."

Now it was Feather's turn to be surprised. The traders in the plaza had seen Montoya intervene outside but had no knowledge of what transpired in the commander's office. He chose his next words carefully. "Perhaps there were those who did not understand the orders."

"Perhaps," Montoya acknowledged. His mind flashed to the missing Marquez; the man had always exhibited a penchant for cruelty.

"What does the Colonel desire?" The Indian leader decided it wise to change subjects.

"He hopes you will send traders to Santa Fe when your gardens are producing again. There's a new group of soldiers and they are getting tired of salted pork from a barrel. They don't want to turn into javelinas!" The friar's face wrinkled in a smile. "Colonel Rodriguez told me to assure you he wishes peace; your people will be treated with respect."

"Very well, before long our traders will return."

Talk turned to other matters. The priest said nothing about the missing soldiers and Feather was careful not to disclose where his village had taken refuge, or mention anything about the captured horses. After the traditional exchanging of gifts, Feather had several men accompany the visitors halfway to Santa Fe.

When Montoya reported that Feather made no mention of further conquistador harassment, under his gentle probing, Rodriguez came to the conclusion that Marquez had simply become tired of duty in the remote outpost and deserted with his group of malcontents.

CHAPTER 56

Parting

Almost a year after coming north, his five Aztec companions approached Cuto about returning home. Xpil, Tenoch, and Patli had decided to resume their life as farmers, declaring that they had experienced more than enough adventure for the time being! Coyotl and Mazatl would accompany them on the trip, but intended to marry their childhood sweethearts and bring them back to the canyon. They asked to borrow horses for the journey.

"With horses, Mazatl and I can be back in less than two months," said Coyotl. "We will teach our wives to ride while we're home and use the fifth horse to bring back supplies."

Cuto and Ria agreed, suggesting that they take the donkeys as well since they were just getting fat and would be useful to the villagers. A few days later the five set out, with Swallow accompanying them as far as the pueblo. After visiting her parents she was to bring back a couple of warriors to help guard the canyon and learn to ride.

The girl returned in a week with Walks in the Grass and Backward Looking. Both men had distinguished themselves in the battle at the pueblo, earning the first chance to learn horsemanship. They were Cuto's age and had received their names because of habits developed as toddlers.

By now, Ria had built several training courses near the houses. Laid out with rock cairns, they were designed to develop agility in the horses and balance for the riders. The two Indians began slowly, walking their mounts through the patterns for days before progressing to a trot and finally to a gentle canter. Both were good students and quickly learned Ria's quiet style with the animals.

The warriors chaffed at the chance to use the advanced course, particularly as they watched the three others practice it at a dead run. The course entailed three thick posts, varying in height from three to six feet, sunk in the ground at intervals over 100 yards. The top of each post was flat and could accommodate a target ranging in size from an orange to a melon.

The objective was to run the course at full speed and attempt to hit one or more of the targets with arrow, spear, or sling. If using a bow, both hands had to be free to operate the weapon; reloading the sling or atlatl for a second shot required astounding hand-eye coordination. In all cases, the rider had to continue guiding the horse with leg pressure and body position while both hands were otherwise occupied.

With Ria's coaching, the two Indians began to develop skills and were soon staying aboard their horses throughout each course. The next step was learning to guide their horses without hands. It took weeks before they were given weapons for the target course. Countless runs were made, and countless arrows fired, before the first melon was knocked off a post.

"We are becoming great fighters!" Walks in the Grass exclaimed as he jumped off to retrieve the large melon skewered by his arrow.

"In time, perhaps." Ria laughed. "For now, let's keep practicing!"

Then she accelerated to full speed, exploding two lemons with her sling before finishing the course.

The Indians looked at each other.

"Some day we will ride like that!" Backward Looking cried with admiration.

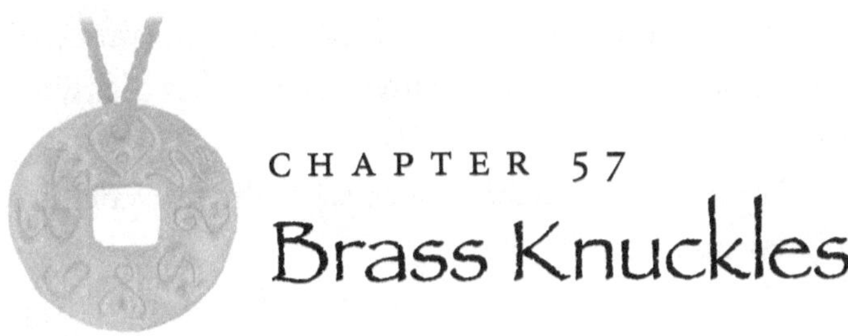

Brass Knuckles

THE PHONE RANG.

"Hello." Great Grandfather jerked the receiver away from his ear as Juan's voice screamed at him.

"It happened again! I can't believe it, it happened again!"

"For heaven's sake, calm down, you almost blew out my eardrum! What happened, another avalanche?" It was early March and he wondered whether the kids had word of another avalanche on Wolf Creek Pass.

"No, it's about the tournament! The Regionals we won last weekend."

"Yes, I was there. You played your heart out!"

"Thank you, Great Grandfather, but that's not why I'm calling. Something happened today! Can we come over?"

"It's Wednesday night, what about homework?" The old man always emphasized the importance of getting schoolwork done immediately when the twins got home.

"I finished it at school because of the team picture in Alamosa."

Great Grandfather remembered that a photographer from the Denver newspaper had come south to get shots of all the winning teams from last week's tournament.

The Center Middle School team, undersized as always against the bigger schools, had miraculously advanced to the finals on the inspired play of Juan and two of his best friends, Adrian and Fidel. An extraordinary 3-point shot by Adrian, with 4 seconds remaining, had secured the win against the same Alamosa team they had beaten in the fall. It was the first time in 30 years that the Center team had won the tournament and almost its entire population had attended the game!

"Okay, come on over."

After giving his consent, the old man barely had time to get cookies on the table before there was a knock on the front door. The twins had obviously sprinted all the way in their excitement. Juan could hardly wait until they were settled before blurting out his news.

"Go back to last fall, when we won the game in Alamosa on my free throws after I got hurt. Remember some older kids made threats about what would happen if we won the Regionals?"

"I do recall something about that."

"Following the photo session today, our team went to get hamburgers and milkshakes for the ride home. Adrian, Fidel, and I let everyone order first and ended up walking a block behind the others on the way back to the bus. All of a sudden a lowered, black, suv pulled up to the curb and six guys jumped out. Each was wearing a black leather jacket with a red skull and crossbones on the back; they were gang members.

"'We warned you last fall, but you didn't listen' said one who was wearing a black dew rag; his eyebrows came together over his nose and he had a scraggly Fu Manchu mustache, 'you embarrassed our boys again. Time for payback!'"

"He grabbed Adrian and started pushing him into an ally. These guys were much bigger than us and I was really scared! Two others reached for Fidel and me but I swung my hamburger sack into the face of one and threw my milkshake at the head of the other, screaming for Fidel to run. Then I found myself charging the leader, driving my shoulder into him and smashing his body against the ally wall. Adrian ducked free and took off but, before I could get up from tackling the guy, the others shoved me down and kneeled on me.

"The leader stood up and, man, was he mad! Blood was streaming off the tip of his nose from a gash in his forehead. He pulled a pair of brass knuckles from his jacket and told the ones holding me down to pin me against the wall.

"'You'll regret that for the rest of your life,' he spat, wiping blood off his face with the back of his hand before slipping the brass knuckles on, 'they'll never be able to repair your nose when I'm done!'

"They yanked me to my feet and rammed me against the wall. He was about to deck me when I saw his eyes flick down from my face.

"'What have we here?' he sneered.

"I looked down and realized that somehow the medallion had popped halfway out of my sweatshirt. It must have happened when I was jerked to my feet; I could feel it resting against the lower part of my throat.

"'This looks like silver and a big piece at that; worth a lot of money I'd say. I'll just appropriate it before it gets all bloody. You don't mind do you?' With a nasty laugh he grabbed the medallion and tried to snap it off my neck.

"Great Grandfather! It was just like what happened with Adzul at the waterfall! As soon as his hand closed over the silver he screamed and lunged backward, dragging me with him in spite of the guys holding me. He shook his hand hard, frantically trying to get rid of the medallion, pulling me this way and that, but it stuck to his flesh and his hand began to smoke! It was the one wearing the brass knuckles and they got so hot from touching the silver they started to glow! He begged help but it must have hurt so bad that finally all he could do was scream. One of the other guys grabbed the cord in one hand and the leader's wrist in the other. It took all his strength to pull the medallion free and it snapped back against my chest.

"The leader was bent over moaning, clutching the burned hand to his stomach; the others stood around looking scared and not knowing what to do. On impulse, I flipped the cord off my neck and started toward them with the medallion thrust forward in my right hand.

"'Leave us alone,' I shouted, 'or you'll get the same thing!'"

"That freaked them out and they all ran to the car, roaring away just as Adrian, Fidel, and our two coaches came running."

There was silence in the room for a full minute after Juan finished the story. Then Great Grandfather leaned forward and fixed the boy with a piercing gaze.

"First, I am extremely proud of you for stepping in to save the other boys. That was not easy considering the odds you faced; it took both courage and character. You are certainly worthy to wear the medallion."

He straightened up, eyes twinkling and a smile wreathing his face.

"Second, it should be clear to all of us that no one outside this family is meant to possess that piece of silver! Now, off with the two of you, tomorrow's a school day and we'll continue the story Saturday morning."

<h1>CHAPTER 58</h1>

Visitors

THE CARCASS OF A DEER was slung across the withers of each horse as Cuto and Walks in the Grass rode up the main canyon one afternoon. When they came in sight of the sentry rocks, the medallion suddenly became warm on Cuto's chest and he reined in his horse.

"What is it?" The Indian kept his voice low.

"I'm not sure, there may be danger."

They rode slowly forward, eyes searching the terrain. In front of them, grassy meadows stretched almost to the sentry rocks; 200 yards to the right a line of cottonwoods marked the stream. The medallion remained warm, just as it had during Cuto's first visit to Santa Fe.

"I don't think an attack is imminent," he said, "but we need to be careful."

"There, along the creek," muttered Walks in the Grass.

In line with the passageway to their canyon, three brush huts had been built under the trees bordering the creek. They hadn't been there that morning when the two set out hunting. Five men stood staring at the riders; they were of medium height and stocky, dressed in long-sleeved cotton shirts, loincloths, and knee-high leather moccasins. All wore headbands. No weapons were in sight.

"Apache." Walks in the Grass spat out the word.

"Let's see if they have approached Backward Looking," said Cuto, heading toward the sentry rocks.

"They appeared several hours ago," reported the watchman, slipping out of the rocks. "After building the huts they stayed in camp, as though awaiting your return."

"Do they have horses?" Cuto inquired.

"No. The Apache are like the Kiowa, Comanche, and Paiute: none have horses. The Pueblo will be the first to own horses!" he announced with pride.

"Have you seen others?"

"No. I slipped into the valley while they were building the huts and warned Ria and Swallow to get to the rim, in case they attacked. The Apache are enemies of the Pueblo."

Cuto noticed that Backward Looking was carrying two lances and had two quivers filled with arrows on his back. He had been prepared to sell his life dearly.

"One of them is approaching." Walks in the Grass interrupted.

A single Apache had left the huts and was walking toward them with a blanket over his right arm. When he had covered roughly half the distance, he stopped and shook out the blanket then sat on it cross-legged facing them.

"He wants to talk." Cuto slid off his horse and handed the reins to Walks in the Grass. "Hang the deer at the houses and stake out the horses nearby. Then get your weapons and come back."

"You can't do this to us!" cried Juan as Great Grandfather stopped talking and stared at the twins with a twinkle in his eye.

"What?" said the old man innocently, although he knew precisely the reason for the outburst.

"Leave us hanging in suspense like that! It's not fair!"

"Oh, you mean pausing the story until next Saturday?" His eyes widened as though he just realized what he had done.

Sophia had hands on hips and a mock frown on her face. "You always time it to end at an exciting part. It's very hard on our nerves!"

"Just trying to toughen you up." Great Grandfather chuckled. "See you next week!"

C H A P T E R 5 9

Palaver

As he unwrapped the sling from his waist and loaded it, the Aztec casually glanced up. Sure enough, he could just make out two heads on the rim; Ria and Swallow were poised to help if necessary. He turned and walked slowly toward the seated Indian, the shortened sling swinging gently at his side.

Stopping 30 feet away, he stared at the other man. There was no expression on the Apache's square brown face whose black eyes, after flicking briefly to the strange weapon hanging from Cuto's right hand, stared impassively at him. It was hard to tell the man's age but the long black hair, held in place by a faded red headband, contained a touch of gray; clearly this was no youngster. A full minute passed with neither breaking the stare. Finally, the Apache swung his left hand in front of him, palm up, indicating Cuto should join him on the blanket.

As he stepped forward, the Aztec dropped the loaded pouch to the ground and paid out the straps so the sling lay extended behind him and could be brought into play from his sitting position. He noted that the other man carried no weapon other than a knife thrust through his belt. After a pause, the Apache broke the silence in a language Cuto didn't recognize.

"I don't understand. Do you speak the language of the Pueblo?"

"I do but we will not speak the words of that people. They are my enemies. We will talk with hands." The harsh voice was filled with disdain.

"As you wish." Cuto said and then signed. "Why have you come?"

"We heard that you defeated many soldiers."

"We had only a small part," Cuto answered. "The Pueblos defeated them at their village."

"A patrol disappeared in this canyon."

"The Spaniards send out many patrols." He had no idea what the Apache knew and had no intention of revealing anything that would endanger his home or family. These men might even be working for the conquistadors, although he doubted it.

"Our scouts saw them enter this canyon but neither they, nor their horses, ever came out."

"Perhaps they left by another way."

The Apache gave a faint smile. "We posted lookouts. The patrol did not come back."

Cuto shrugged.

"The Spaniards are careful to protect their horses," signed the Indian. "Yet you are riding two of them. The patrol had many more."

"You did not come here to discuss the soldiers." Cuto had begun to understand what the Indian was really interested in.

"You speak the truth. It's their horses I seek."

Cuto stared at him, face expressionless.

"The Apache live in small bands. Our only protection from the Long Swords is to hide in the desert. With horses, we could defend ourselves against them." Left unsaid was the idea that they could also attack other Indians, including the Pueblo. "We wish to trade with you."

"If we had horses, what would you offer in trade?"

"The yellow rock that the soldiers seek."

The younger man shrugged. "We have no use for it and if the Spaniards found out, they would come in force and kill all of us. Why don't you take it to them directly?"

There was a pause. "In the beginning, the soldiers were cruel to us in their obsession with the yellow rock. Despite their tortures, we never told them where to find it. We would die rather than give it to them."

Cuto thought for several minutes. He knew the Indian tribes in the area were enemies of one another but he also knew they all had a common enemy in the soldiers. At length he made a decision.

"I understand your words. Far away the soldiers were cruel to my people also and, because we fought on foot, we couldn't defeat them. With enough horses for battle, the tribes can break the power of the conquistadors. I have a few, you have seen two of them, but it is not enough. It will take time to build a herd. I suggest you raid the soldiers for horses; it's the fastest way to get them. But, if you are fearful of the Spaniards, come again in two years and I will trade you a stallion and a mare to begin your own herd."

The man's eyes glittered in anger and a scowl came over his face. "We fear no one and we need horses now!"

"Your fathers and grandfathers, and their fathers before them, did not have these animals yet they managed to survive in this land. There is time. Since you are the first to come, I will trade with no Apache before you."

Cuto saw a flash of malevolence as the Indian's eyes bored into his, but it was quickly subdued as the brave stood up.

"We will return in two years."

Gathering his blanket, he strode back toward the creek. The other four surrounded him for a moment before they all entered one of the huts.

CHAPTER 60

Skirmish

CUTO LAY ON HIS BACK in the main canyon 50 yards from the sentry rocks, loaded sling at hand, staring at the brilliant stars in a moonless sky. Far away a pack of coyotes yipped in the night and a few crickets chirped in the grass around him; otherwise it was totally still. He wondered whether his friends' suspicions were justified.

Upon hearing about the meeting, Walks in the Grass had stated flatly, "The Apache won't wait two years, they'll attack tonight if they think they can overpower us; otherwise, they'll come back later in force."

Backward Looking had concurred. "They're warlike and crave dominance over all other Indians. We had best be prepared."

Thinking of the look he had briefly glimpsed in the eyes of the Apache, Cuto had agreed. If the visitors guessed how short-handed they were, they would surely attack. He had signaled Ria and Swallow to remain on the rim and then gone to the house for his armor shirt, extra spears, and an atlatl. As an afterthought, he tucked a small sack into his shirt.

The fight with Marquez had raised concerns about a night attack; if the Spaniards had entered the passage in the dark, the observers on the rim wouldn't have been able to see them. To counteract the problem, the Aztecs had built two large stacks of wood just outside the entrance, flanking the approach. When ignited, the bonfires would reveal anyone trying to get in. In the event the first line defenders had to retreat, the remaining sidewalls in the fissure had piles of dry wood to set ablaze, exposing the enemy for those above to unleash their deadly rain of rock.

Knowing that the medallion would warn him if the Apaches approached, Cuto had positioned himself to give extra time for lighting the fires. Three hours passed and he was starting to doze when his eyes suddenly flew open as the silver became hot on his skin! The cricket's song had ceased and it was deathly still in the dark. Raising his head slightly, he looked for any movement in the grass around him. He saw nothing, but his ears picked up the faintest whisper of rustling grass 30 feet to his left. The enemy was moving fast and had almost passed him!

For a second he was tempted to race to the rocks to alert the waiting warriors, but he knew the Apaches were so close that any movement would result in an instant attack. He had no way of knowing how many were to either side and would be at a terrible disadvantage, since they would immediately see him outlined against the stars if he stood up.

Realizing that he was nearly invisible at ground level the Aztec remained motionless until the tiniest of sounds revealed that the Apache had passed and was now between him and the sentry rocks. He waited a minute more and then silently stood. In the faint starlight he made out a figure in the grass, 25 feet away, and set his sling in motion.

CHAPTER 61

Mask

As HE ANTICIPATED, the strange noise of the straps whirring through the air froze the man in the grass for an instant and he had time for four powerful revolutions before releasing the rock. There was a distinct 'thud,' followed by a soft groan as the hurtling missile crushed the enemy's ribcage. At the same instant an arrow slammed into his chest with such force that he staggered backward. But for the armor shirt, it would have passed almost entirely through his body!

"Light the fires," shouted Cuto, reloading the sling and turning to race away toward the stream. Arrows from both sides slammed into his back, knocking him flat, but he stumbled up and ran. His Incan armor had saved his life again; the five men had been closer than he thought and he had been an easy target when he stood up. He covered 10 more yards before a searing pain erupted in his right thigh and the leg collapsed, throwing him again to the ground. He felt for the arrow. It had entered the back of his thigh and was sticking out the front.

Cuto knew the Apaches would be on him momentarily. Flames were already lighting the night as he struggled to stand. Reaching for the rock pouch at his belt, his hand brushed the leather bag inside his shirt and he smiled grimly in the dark. He might gain a small advantage and make them pay before he went down. It only took seconds to open the sack and slip its contents over his head and then he was up, the loaded sling whirling. Clenching teeth against the excruciating pain in his leg, he searched the grass for the enemy.

The two Apaches sent to finish him off slid through the cover on bent legs, to create the least silhouette against the 15-foot flames now rising behind them. They knew the man had been hit by a number of arrows but they weren't sure whether he was dead and kept their bows fully drawn.

With no warning, an apparition rose from the grass 25 feet away. Both men were seasoned warriors but involuntarily froze in confusion as superstition crowded out all other thoughts. Highlighted by the roaring fires behind them was a jaguar, ears flattened in the lethal position of anger, possessing the body of a man! So startling was the sight that neither moved for an instant, mesmerized by the specter.

Their hesitation was fatal. The man to Cuto's left went down without a sound as a baseball-sized rock hit him directly between the eyes at 100 MPH. Ignoring the incredible pain in his leg, the Aztec gave his best imitation of a jaguar's roar and advanced toward the other man while reloading his sling with lightning speed. The Apache fired his arrow instinctively. But the roar, muffled though it was by the mask, was unmistakable and when the arrow fell harmlessly from the man-chest, his nerve broke and he ran. Outlined in the flames he was an easy target and fell before covering five yards, the vertebra at the base of his neck shattered.

CHAPTER 62
Confusion

When the sentries set fire to the tinder-dry wood, it flamed high into the air. Looking down from the rim, Ria and Swallow could clearly see the bare ground in front of the entrance in the light of the twin blazes.

"There!" whispered Swallow. "Over to the left, I thought I saw movement just beyond the firelight."

"I saw it too," replied Ria. "And there was something moving on the right side. They're skulking in the darkness."

"There were five this afternoon," said the girl. "That accounts for only two, where are the others?"

"Backward Looking and Walks in the Grass must be hidden inside the passage but I thought there was a shout from out in the dark where Cuto was lying, just before they lit the fires." There was a catch in Ria's voice. "He may be trapped out there."

In fact, Cuto was searching the ground between him and the fires for the two remaining enemies. Something caught his eye a few yards to the right and he spun, mindless of the pain, ready to fire. Against the flames a figure rose, facing away from the Aztec and crouching, knife in hand, as if to attack someone on the ground in front of him. The figure took a step before suddenly stumbling and falling face forward, as first one arrow and then another flashed up into his body. Unsure whether the downed man was friend or foe, Cuto kept the sling whirling at full speed until he saw Backward Looking rise out of the grass and stare at the body.

Lowering the sling, Cuto limped forward to greet his friend. He was startled to see the Pueblo whip an arrow from his quiver and pull the bow to a full draw, aiming straight at him. Stopping, Cuto held both hands up at shoulder height in surrender. Only when the Indian saw the sling hanging from the right hand did he lower the bow. But his face was twisted in confusion as he stared at the Aztec. In spite of the agony in his right thigh, Cuto laughed aloud.

"I suppose you wondered how a jaguar got into the fight!" he said, pulling off the mask just as the leg finally gave out and he slumped to the ground.

CHAPTER 63
Missing

Two weeks later, Cuto was sitting on the stallion near the sentry rocks while the others put horses through new maneuvers that Ria had designed nearby. His thigh was heavily bandaged, and he still walked with a decided limp, but the leg felt better every day. Backward Looking's quick action in cutting the arrowhead off and extracting the shaft, plus his wife's skill with healing herbs and poultices, had resulted in a steady recovery.

Concerning the skirmish, he had learned that the two Pueblo warriors split up after lighting the fires—knowing it was five against one out in the darkness. Backward Looking slipped past the sentry rocks and circled to find him. Walks in the Grass stayed to slow any attempt by the enemy to gain the entrance, knowing there was help from above if needed.

Backward Looking had been so stealthy he had literally tripped over a warrior lying beside a clump of sagebrush just beyond the firelight. The man had reacted like a striking rattlesnake, springing out of the grass with his knife slashing at the Pueblo. The latter had managed to hold on to his loaded bow as he fell and got the shot off from his back as the Apache loomed over him. Hit in the chest, the Apache was still coming when Backward Looking transfixed him with a second arrow. When Cuto materialized out of the darkness, he had automatically notched another arrow.

"All I could think was, 'What kind of medicine do these Apaches possess!' I was so keyed up my fingers were actually starting to release the bowstring when I saw your sling; I almost had to shoot the arrow into the ground!" Backward Looking had the rest of them laughing as he described the incident.

"It's pretty shocking to encounter a jaguar-man materializing out of the night." Walks in the Grass had sympathized with a grin.

In the back of their minds, however, was a nagging concern about the Apache leader. Despite a careful search of the canyon the following day, they had found no trace of him. The four other bodies lay where they fell but he had vanished without a trace. The warriors surmised the man knew they would use horses to chase him down and was careful to leave no trail. They knew that sooner or later he would be back.

CHAPTER 64

Reunion

CUTO WATCHED THE OTHERS run their mounts at full speed through the obstacle courses, bending, turning, and reversing direction with agility he couldn't have imagined when they first rode into the canyon. A flicker of movement far down valley caught his attention. He edged the black a few yards away from the rocks so that he had a full view of the canyon. The motion came again, almost two miles away. Focusing intently, he was sure he saw riders!

A touch of his heels sent the black speeding toward the others.

"Riders coming!" His alarm rang out and all activity ceased as everyone whirled their mounts around to stare down valley. The tell-tale glint of sun on armor would send them all racing toward the cleft to take up defensive positions.

"There are eight horses." Walks in the Grass had the sharpest eyes. "But only four riders."

There was silence as they waited, each trying to sort out the puzzling news. The conquistadors would have a much larger force and every horse would have been mounted. The only other explanation could be four Indian warriors, each with a spare horse, but where would they have gotten horses? Had the Apaches overcome their fear and raided Santa Fe?

As the distance slowly closed, they could make out more detail.

"One of the riders is leading a packhorse," reported Walks in the Grass. "Three horses are trailing in the rear, heads down."

"It's Coyotl and Mazatl! They're bringing their wives!" cried Ria, suddenly sprinting her horse toward the distant figures. The others followed in a happy canter to greet their old friends and before long the whole group was making its way slowly toward the sentry rocks, laughing and sharing the news. Ria had grown up with Itzel and Sacnite and introduced them to Swallow. In no time the four were chattering away like sisters.

Mazatl emotionally narrated that Adzul had died peacefully in his sleep two months before. It followed an afternoon hunt where he dropped three quail in succession with perfect headshots from his sling. He was reported to have said he hoped his grandson would be able to do the same when he was almost 100. Cuto smiled, fondly remembering his countless unsuccessful attempts to sneak up on his grandfather. The old warrior had always set the standard for him!

"Where did you find the three extra horses?" inquired Ria, noting the listless behavior of the new arrivals.

"They appeared at our camp four nights ago." Coyotl explained. "They must have smelled the creek and wanted to join our animals. All were saddled and bridled; one had a piece of picket rope still looped around its neck. From their condition, they must have wandered in the desert for several days. We threw away the equipment and brought them along. If past history is any measure, I suspect rest and a good grass diet will do wonders." Ria nodded in agreement.

Although the piles of wood had been rebuilt, there were plenty of ashes in evidence around the entry to the passage and the returning Aztecs were impressed by the success of the fires during the Apache attack. They all stopped to hear the details of that night and admire the new, 10-foot high stacks.

"They look big enough to keep the whole area lit all night!" Mazatl marveled.

"Possibly, if fired at intervals," acknowledged Backward Looking. "The light was a great help because the Apache are extremely dangerous in the dark. Without the fires they could have easily taken us."

After a good laugh at Backward Looking's confusion over the jaguar mask, they rode into the corridor one by one, the new horses dutifully following.

Emerging into the hidden valley, Itzel and Sacnite gasped. Stretching away on either side, towering cliffs were awash in red from the setting sun. In front of them three adobe houses lined a murmuring creek shaded by tall cottonwood trees. Each house was ringed with a colorful bed of flowers and backed up to a series of tidy garden plots separated by low earthen walls, Aztec style. Water bubbled along cleverly designed channels from the stream to irrigate the vegetables.

Through a break in the trees they could see a small herd of horses 100 yards away, grazing peacefully in green grass not far from a cluster of deer. High above, framed in the deepening blue of the sky, an eagle cruised currents along the rim searching for prey in the meadows.

"You never told me it was like this," an awestruck Itzel murmured to Coyotl, while Sacnite looked at Mazatl in disbelief.

The two men sat on their horses, staring at the scene with happy smiles.

"You'd never have believed us," laughed Coyotl. "Welcome home!"

The Heirs of the Medallion
Lita
Book 3

Intrigued by reports of a vast body of water to the north and west, Cuto's grandchildren Lita and her brother Rutu leave the family home in the canyon near Santa Fe to pursue a yearlong quest. On the eve of their departure Lita, as the youngest family member, receives the ancient silver medallion from her grandfather, who is now almost 90.

After months of adventure, the pair is attacked by a war party of Indians far to the north. Trapped on a hilltop, vastly out-numbered and with Rutu incapacitated, Lita knows she must fight to the death to protect the secret of the medallion.